Her name is Jana Jay. She and her boys have a mission in life to help others whether they are alive or not. She had a vision of mirrors and almost lost part of herself. What she sees makes all of them want to rescue those who are stuck in a mirror realm. It's definitely a supernatural issue. Spirits or people usually come to them for help and they know what to do. This is different, and they need a plan ... then life interferes. They each have their own gifts and use them to protect those abused by the dead or those who are their masters, but who's protecting them?

DOUBLE MIRROR

SHIVERS SERIES

MIKI WARD
GARRETT WARD

Cover Design by Christina Schneider at Miki and Mine LLC
Editing by Michelle Hoffman
Copyright © 2018 Miki Ward & Garrett V Ward
Published by Miki & Mine LLC
All rights reserved.
ISBN-13: 978-1-949250-10-7
Published in the United States of America

NOTE FROM THE AUTHORS

We dedicate this book to our Mom
-Miki & Garrett

TO OUR READERS ...

Thank you for purchasing this book and reading it! I hope you, as the reader, enjoy this book as much as we enjoyed writing it. This is book two of our Shivers Series. Book one is called We See You. Trigger warning; be warned, this book contains: reverse harem relationships, graphic sex scenes, violence, paranormal events, and language.

Sincerely Yours,
Miki Ward and Garrett Ward

FINDING JANA

*J*ana Sue Jay sits on her bed, alone in her room, in front of her vanity, absentmindedly stroking her silky golden-brown hair with a sterling silver brush, guiding it with her other hand. This is her favorite brush, it was a present from her boys, Greydan, Kaden, JoeJoe, and Asa, when she turned sixteen.

The young clairvoyant replays the last day like watching a movie. She captures each moment, immersing herself in the memory. The relief of finding and rescuing the Gordon kids is still fresh. Although satisfying, it's left her drained. Yet, if you think she isn't ready for another chance to help others, you don't know her. She's a fighter.

Jana stiffens as she feels one of her visions coming on. She hurries to her bed and lies down just in time for it to claim her. She's ready and falls into the dream state. Her stomach lurches at the literal drop. She sees a mirror as she continues downward to her destination. No, there's not just one mirror; there are many, and they spread into the dark infinity of space.

Jana stops in front of one of the mirrors and sets her feet

onto a smooth floor. She reaches out a hand to brush the surface of the outermost pane of the mirror.

"What the heck is this?"

It has no definite boundary. Her fingers sink in slightly. She jerks them back instinctively with a squeak. Something touched her! The young clairvoyant hears a cackling, demented laughter, it's growing in intensity. Shivers run down her spine as she realizes she isn't alone. She senses there are more here than the one who's laughing. These beings are distinct and apart from the crazy loon who's glee-fully cackling like a wicked witch from a bad movie. The crazy 'thing' is happy and wants his prey, Jana, to join them all in the hidden place behind the glass.

It says over and over, "Come back, I just want to talk to you. Please, come back. I'm so lonely."

The hair raises on Jana's arms as she figures out the other personalities are fighting for her attention, too. The sound is distorted, whispered, and they're all speaking at once. She shakes her head to clear it, wondering if the crazy 'thing' wants her to know the others are here. Concentrating, she's shocked to register the others in this mysterious realm are here against their will, she's sure of it.

Jana stops dead in her tracks. She learned a long time ago not to strike out on her own, she needs her crew to operate in the paranormal. She can enter the mirror in front of her alone, but her group works best together. They're stronger together and have been since they met in kindergarten. This is a job for all of them. She won't attempt it alone, no matter how tempting it is.

Her heart throbs, she's panting, and shakes with the need to help the prisoners! The presence is tempting her, a phys-ical demand, beseeching her to enter the mirror. Again resisting, she jerks her shoulders up like a fighter's bracing stance and forces herself to grit out, "I don't operate in the supernatural without my guys! They keep her strong, especially when it's creepy, then hold her together when she reaches a breaking point. They're her best friends as well as her boyfriends.

She would die for Greydan, JoeJoe, Kayden, and Asa. No one is as close to her, not even her parents who are lovely people. They've got hectic lives and tend to let her live her own life. She's proven to them that she can be trusted, so they give her a lot of freedom. She's their one and only baby born in their later years, a miracle, one they had given up having. Her life may not be like everyone else's, but it fits her. She's made good decisions for herself no matter how different her ways might be from the 'normal' of most people.

Jana moves out of the vision with resolve. Her body's normal reaction every time is a high libido that the boys help alleviate. This is strange, though; she finds she can't move a muscle. She opened her eyes, sure she's awake and in her body, but it isn't responding. The supernatural is always exerting itself on her, but this is different; she usually has some control. Something happened when she touched the mirror. She snatched her hand away... just not fast enough. Thinking back, she knows she heard creepy laughter and a voice. ... What did it say?

Jana can see parts of her room without turning her head. The top of her vanity, the closed door, and her light are in view. She's lying on her bed, wrapped in a towel. She had left her family and the boys downstairs finishing their breakfast, to take a shower. When she got out she fell into the vision and was lured by the voices to enter the mirror realm.

She's positive she couldn't have plunged into the trance more than ten minutes ago. Her pulse is racing. *You can't panic. Think! What happened?* Ordinarily adept at understanding her visions, fear is slowing her response. She doesn't give up, though, that isn't who she is. *I must have left part of me in that damn mirror. Is it possible that 'thing' touching me sucked out a part of me?*

Need for her to move is threatening to swamp her senses and making her angry. She trembles as her body cools. *At least I'm getting dry lying here ... freaking paralyzed.*

Jana's in and out of consciousness and starts to phase out and sleep, unable to control the lethargy. She's confident the boys will help when they find her. *Someone sneak up here and check on me!* She drifts off, waking again in a floating haze. She hears someone coming with loud steps on the stairs bringing hope to her clouded mind.

"Jana?" she hears a light knock on her door.

Her heart flutters at the sound of Kaden so close knowing she isn't dressed. She needs him to touch her! So frustrating!

"Jana?" This time the knock is louder. "Jana, I'm coming in!"

The door creaks, and Kaden glances inside. He spots Jana lying on the bed unmoving and rushes to her side, "What the hell? Jana are you all right?" He touches his girl's cold hand and leans over her.

She understands his worry as relief floods her, and her stiff unmoving spine relaxes.

Kaden moves closer, and he stares into her golden-brown eyes, "Jana talk to me. What's wrong, sug? I see your eyes move. Why isn't the rest of your body moving? Sugar, blink if you can hear me, then I'll know what's working."

Did I blink? How would I know? Jana Jay, fight your way out of this and get yourself moving before all the boys get worried and try to do something brave to save you.

"I'm going to get Asa and the others. I'll be back real quick, sugar," Kaden says, covering her with the throw blanket from the end of the bed. He kisses her on the head. He doesn't make it out the door before Asa, Greyd, and

JoeJoe come into view. Earlier, Asa had heard her asking for someone to sneak up and had sent Kaden. Then not wanting to miss any time with his girl, he came, too, and they all headed up. They cram into Jana's room and see that she isn't moving. Together, they ask, "What's wrong?"

Asa is next to Jana in a flash, his breath hot on her ear as he whispers, "What's wrong, honey?"

She thinks an answer to him. *"I'm so glad you can hear my thoughts! I had a vision when I got out of the shower. Here's everything I saw and felt in the vision before I get too groggy and fall to sleep on you."* Jana sends her handsome mind reader as detailed a picture as she can muster. *"I think something changed me when I touched that mirror. My fingers sunk into it a little, and something touched me. I really want to go back. That's crazy, I know, but it's hard to not go back. It seems like the desire is even greater now that you're all here with me. I think it's because I know I would be safer... no... I've got to quit thinking that."*

Asa faces the others and says, "What happened is … she had a vision in this land of mirrors, and it's affecting her. She touched the glass, and something touched her from the other side when her fingers sunk in."

They're all talking at once, Asa is filtering it all. He's that way, the stuff people think and say just makes sense to him no matter how fast it comes at him. Jana tells him he's a genius and not just another pretty face. She still unquestioningly likes his face no matter what. Who wouldn't? He's hot with gorgeous brown hair and crystal-green eyes. He's a dazzling man, and they have a seriously close relationship. He is a model. Well, at least since he took a part-time position at a local modeling agency. Asa only models on weekends, no matter how hard his agent tries to make him work during the week. Asa's already making a name for himself, even though his parents don't have a clue. They're never home to know. They're missionaries. They love their son, they've just got their own lives and little ability to have contact with him. This is especially true when they're in the more remote areas of the world.

Greydan asserts his leadership with the group, "Calm down, guys. We can get Jana to take us to the mirror. Then if you'll read it, JoeJoe, you can tell Kaden what to do, so he can manipulate the thing that hurt her into releasing whatever part of her it kept. Just don't let anything in there touch you. Asa, can you make sure she heard me and ask if she'll take us into her crazy vision, now?"

"Yes, I'm on it," Asa answers, his elf-like features fearful for his sweetheart. The five of them have been friends since they were five years old when they learned they each had paranormal talents. They all have a unique gift that they call physic abilities and have bonded by using them to help others.

Once the boys found out Jana could see visions, they discovered a way to see them with her. It took years, and they still can only do it with her driving the bus. They've been building the ability to go with her just like a muscle. It's easier now than the first time they tried, but none of them can do it without their girl.

"Jana," Asa says in a low tone, "can you take us with you, into the vision?"

"Yes, but you might have to wake me up if I drift off again. It is hard to stay awake, Elf Boy."

She's been calling him 'Elf Boy' since the first time they met and sat together at their little group desk. *The Fellowship of the Ring* movie was popular at the time. Asa hides nothing with his facial expressions, particularly when she calls him that. She isn't hiding the feelings she has for him, either, as she gazes into his eyes. The whole crew cares deeply for each other, and it shows. "We're going to prepare for you to take us into your visual memory. Let me tell the others," he replies.

He turns and shares, "She said that she might fall asleep because it's hard for her to stay awake, so we need to watch for that when we get relaxed and ready."

Greydan takes over, "Okay, you guys get comfortable. I'll start the process." They had come across a book on hypnosis when they were younger, and were experimenting. They found Jana could take them into a vision or dream. It was an accident but a good one. They've tried different ways, but the vision travel never works if one of them is missing.

Kaden is the quickest of the guys to start relaxing. He sits on the floor at Jana's feet and leans against her bed with his shoulder touching her leg. Greydan sits similarly on the other side of her legs, but still touching her. JoeJoe is the biggest and lies on the bed, perpendicular to her and lifts her head and shoulders to his lap before leaning back on the wall and closing his eyes. Asa lies near her side, but with his legs diagonal, so they don't block Greydan sitting on the floor. He puts his hand on her waist, hoping for as much contact as he can. They relax and prepare themselves for the next part of the process

2

SHARING THE VISION

"*E*veryone relax your minds and bodies," Greydan says calmly to his friends as they sink into the exercise for vision traveling with Jana. It's become effortless for them, due to years of practice. Each of them quickly relaxes, and he continues, "Start at your feet. Breathe deeply in through your mouth and out through your nose. Feel your feet relax, then legs and move to your hands, arms, and shoulders. All of your troubles are leaving your awareness as you focus on Jana. Don't worry, she'll be here for you in a few seconds. Just wait, then we'll be together in the dream realm of her vision." Greydan always leads them through this little meditative exercise. They don't really need it spoken anymore, but when it comes to their girl, they take no chances and follow their routine.

They reach a trancelike state in minutes. Greydan's gentle voice trails off as he enters the dream world and watches Jana walk toward him. He smiles at her spirit self. She looks the same as her physical body but even sexier as the light around her glitters with gold sparkles. They're in an area that looks more like a set of a horror movie than a group rendezvous venue. The air surrounding them is thick and filled with gray smoke.

Greydan's relieved when she says, "Greyd, over this way. Stay with me while I connect with the others." Jana uses her nickname for Greydan, her star football player. Others use the nickname, but it never sounds as good. Jana turns and walks a few steps. The scene doesn't change, but he's sure they are in a different location.

"This place feels different," he says.

After Jana connects with each of her boys, she retells what she felt and saw in this metaphysical state. Jana can show them her vision here, so she does.

Asa, who can read minds says, "The entity who spoke to her is definitely hostile. It has evil intentions toward you, Jana." He pauses briefly, looking protectively at her before he continues, "That thing wants to suck all your energy into itself, so it can use it to get to the material realm where we live. I think there are others, but they're too far away for me to tell what they're thinking."

Kaden speaks up, "I'm glad you are okay, sugar, will you take JoeJoe and me to the mirrors, so we can read them? I'll see if I can tell the thing or demon whatever it is to leave you alone and give you back what it took or is controlling."

Kaden is the manipulator of the group. He can tell someone to do something, and they do it without question. Even his crew and Jana do what he says. They laugh sometimes and make a game of it, but he's careful not to abuse his gift. It's his thought that if he misuses it, it'll get taken away, and he likes it. His character wouldn't let him bully others with it, anyhow. He's confident and leaves Jana no question but to agree. She stares into his cognac-brown eyes and melts. Her mouth dry, she agrees with a nod. They stay in one place, but the area around them changes again as it did while Jana was connecting with each of them. In a split second, they're surrounded by heavy horizontal and vertical lines of light. They gaze around, searching the area.

Greydan speaks first and says precisely where they are, "Guys, we're in a giant infinity mirror." His hands are waving through the air trying to locate a solid surface.

Jana replies, "Greyd, we see it, only it's over here. ..." There is a general murmur as she points out the location of the infinity mirror. They are all seeing many false—what appear to be hallways with lines of light.

That's when Asa stops them with a gasp, "Guys, wait. The monster wants us all to see the mirror differently. It's creating false images to fool us. Kaden, you're the manipulator. It's up to you to make this thing show us the correct mirror."

"I'm on it," Kaden says. His eyes search the area as he says, "We know you're here. Take away the illusions and extra mirrors." As he finishes the lines become less confusing and come together in one specific location. Kaden walks the few steps to the edge of the mirror and motions for JoeJoe to come to him. This mirror has depth and appears 3D with lights forming sections resembling the hallways they saw before.

JoeJoe moves forward and reaches a hand out to the outermost section of the mirror. JoeJoe is a psychometrist meaning he can read the history of an object by touching it. He's so gifted at it that he can feel the emotions, smells, and tastes associated with an article, not just the history. He speaks in his deep timber, "I've seen this type of double mirror before. They're used to fool the seer into thinking an image is bigger than it is, making it seem like it recedes into infinity. It fools the eye and can be used in lots of applications, mainly art. Here, though, the builder is trying to fool you into walking forward, so you'll come into contact with his mirror construct and be caught like a spider web catching prey." He doesn't take his hand from the surface and reaches for Kaden. Holding his friend's hand, he continues, "Kaden, we all know when you really want something you can get anyone to do it for you. Do you think you can manipulate this thing, this being, into giving Jana back the piece of her it took now?"

"Let's see," Kaden answers with a confident grin. He concentrates for a second then says out loud, "Give our friend back what you stole. Now!" The atmosphere seems to grow darker still. The room appears to have shrunk.

The group of teens waits. Within seconds, they hear a voice whine, "No, you'll hurt me if I do. Give me your energy. I'll only trade with you."

Jana screams, "Duck, guys!"

None of them wait, they instantly hit the dirt. Okay, it isn't necessarily dirt, they hit the floor, anyway. As they do, a bolt of balled electricity flies over them. Its electrical tendrils reach for them as it flies overhead. Jana leans against Greyd, she's weakened by the ball of electricity. One of its tendrils had raked down the length of her torso. Her warning was timely enough for her to issue an alert to her guys, but it didn't allow her enough time to see them to safety and to protect herself. She wobbles trying to stand back up. Greydan helps her with his strong arms and wraps her in them.

Kaden isn't finished and says again, "No, give her back what you took. I'm getting impatient. No trades."

The disembodied voice says, "Alright, but you will owe me a soul. Move forward and touch the mirror, little Jana." She thinks about it and looks at Asa with a questioning stare from the circle of Greyd's arms.

Asa says, "It thinks that it wants to please Kaden, so it won't hurt you. It really intends to give you your energy back, hun. I don't know how it knows your name."

Greydan says, "As soon as it gives it to you, get us out of here. Don't wait. We'll find out more later."

Everyone holds hands except Jana as she moves forward and lightly touches the glass the way JoeJoe had. Her whole body is enveloped in a glimmer of light with sparkles falling over her. She does just as Greyd asked and grabs his hand then takes them out of the mirror realm in a jiffy. With a guttural moan quickly growing into a screech, the entity realizes what it had just done. It acts immediately to block their flight. But it's too late, Jana Sue Jay has pulled them out of the awful place of mirrors and back into their own bodies before it can retaliate.

Their girl rises up from the bed, a little stiff from the memory of the electrical wound on her side. It's just a memory though, her flesh body is whole and healed. All the boys lean into her in a great big group hug. She gushes, "Thank you for rescuing me. I never want to find out what life is like without you." Their minds and bodies, alive with the thrill of the rescue and escape, they turn their smiling faces to her.

Asa says almost in a pant, "When that thing screamed, I caught its thought that it has decided it will find us and get her back. I also felt others; not just the evil thing, but stolen souls. They're real and being held prisoner on the other side of the mirrors. Every mirror has a soul behind it I don't think they're alive, but they might be; I didn't have enough time to hear more of their thoughts, just that they're prisoners, and it's terrible in there. They were all like Jana was earlier, and were pleading for help like they knew I could hear them."

Jana answered, "I know you're right, Asa. I could feel them. But we really need to do some research, so we can help them. At least I want to help them. What do you guys think? Shall we vote?"

"Yes," most of them answer at once.

JoeJoe is the only one of the boys who did not say yes to helping instantly. He says, "I'll only agree if we can be sure that Jana and you guys will be safe. Otherwise, it has to be something we wait for until we're sure of our safety."

JoeJoe does like to help others but taking chances with his girl or his friends isn't something he stands for. On the other hand, he's known for jumping in the way to save them without a thought to his own safety. Once when they were in grade school, he did that very thing when a bully with a baseball bat cornered Kaden in the parking lot. He had a chipped shoulder blade from the ordeal, but never once complained. The rest of the school year, he walked all of his friends to the parking lot. Now that they're older, he's still doing it; no one intends to stop him. It's his thing.

3

PLANNING BIRTHDAYS

*I*t was just after breakfast when Jana returned to her bedroom to get ready for the day. After their little trip to the double mirror realm, it's now afternoon. On the way out the door with the guys, she pauses to say, "Bye, mom. Bye, dad. We're going to the library to finish up on some research. We'll be back later."

Her dad calls out, "Thanks, sweetheart. I know those guys will keep you safe, but really, stay safe. If you guys need a ride, call!"

Jana laughs, "Thanks, dad, love you."

Being that it's the day after Halloween and school's out for a teacher service day, their little group has the afternoon to themselves. As she'd told her parents, Jana and her boys head to the library. It's cold but not so bad they need to stay bundled up. The sun is out, shining brightly, and no snow is in the forecast for the next few days. It's just going to be cold. But, hey, it's October in upstate New York, what do you expect?

The teens talk excitedly as they walk. Next week is Jana's birthday, and they want to do something special for her, so the boys are grilling her about what she'd like to do and what she wants for her eighteenth.

Jana laughs as she parries their questions, "I have everything I want. Maybe we should have a big party at Greyd's and JoeJoe's house since Asa and Kaden have birthdays this month, too? Yeah, that's what I want. Do you think your mom will go for it, guys?" she asks Greyd and JoeJoe as she swings Kaden's hand back and forth while they walk.

"What? You know our mom, Jana, she'll love the idea," Greyd answers.

As the crew discusses birthday plans, they walk past a department store, and a pretty girl who they all know walks out. She spots Greydan immediately. Then with an icy glance toward Jana, which rivals the frigid temperature, she puts on her most disarming smile and walks directly up to him. "Hi, Greydan. You know the fall formal is after the football game Friday after next, would you like to take me?" She simpers with a pout as her hand gently massages his chest.

Greydan's used being flirted with as the team's star tight-end, but this is too much. His demeanor closes down, and he steps back and away from her outstretched hand. "No, Stacy, I'm taking Jana. You know she's my girlfriend. I'd appreciate it if you would just stop trying to get me to go out with you," he answers with a glance at Jana, just to be sure she's okay. When he meets her golden eyes, she gives him a little wink to calm him, letting him know she doesn't blame him.

Kaden squeezes Jana's hand a little, so she won't feel bad, while hoping to give her a bit more confidence. Funny thing, Jana doesn't even worry a little that Greyd will say yes to Stacy, especially in front of them all. Still, she isn't happy with Stacy Perrin. *How dare she? Greyd is mine. Wait ... if I'm going with Greyd to the fall formal, I should tell my parents I want a beautiful dress for the dance. Maybe that'll be my birthday present from them.* Getting excited as she starts to plan the dance and the birthday party in her head, she smiles and forgets to be angry.

Asa releases a breath, knowing what she's thinking and glad that she isn't jealous … right now at least. Having a friend who knows what you're thinking is natural to all of the crew, and they think nothing of it. For the most part, they don't hide things from each other, and Asa is outstanding about keeping a secret if it comes to that.

Stacy huffs, "Fine, I just thought you might like to feel special. I am the class president! Taking me would be so much better than dating her and just being one of the myriads of followers of the Princess of Planet Weird!" Stacy's voice rises the more she speaks, ending almost in a scream. She starts stomping away before she even finishes savaging Greydan.

The group briefly pauses, taken aback by the sudden and unwanted intrusion. "Don't listen to her, Jana. You're the only girl I've ever liked," Greyd says.

Jana just stares at him for a few uncomfortable heartbeats before she busts out laughing and says, "I can see why she wants you, though!" Suddenly, the cold doesn't seem so cold, and the teens resume their trek to the library.

When the crew arrives at the library, JoeJoe opens the door and holds it for his friends. That's another one of his things; he's very gentlemanly. The young people enter the warmth and quiet of the big room and make their way to an empty table then open notebooks on their phones.

Jana whispers to the boys, "I'm going to start in paranormal research for other realms. Greydan, will you check anything that might pertain to mirrors and spirits? JoeJoe, I saw some books the last time we were here that had information regarding the science and construction of historical mirrors linked to supernatural events, can you start there? I'll show you if you need. Kaden, will you help me? Asa …"

Asa stops her and smiles. "I know. You want me to look into anything that pertains to taking others into other realms involving mirrors, right?" He ends with his signature smile. It makes her weak in the knees every time one of her boys smiles at her like that.

Each of them is busy and engrossed in their assigned task. None of them notice that hours have gone by until JoeJoe's stomach growls loudly. Jana giggles quietly and says under her breath, "We should leave and get some dinner, so we can talk over what we've learned. We can decide what will help to save the mirror prisoners or not and keep looking."

They all nod to her in agreement and get ready to leave. Each of them carries a few books to the front desk to check out. The librarian knows them and takes no notice of their choices but reminds Jana that she needs to reset her pin on her eBook app. "Thank you, Miss Purty, I haven't been able to get it open, can I do that now?" Jana asks, noticing that Asa is frowning. That could mean anything. She'll ask him about it later.

"Sure, you can write it here, and I'll enter it for you," the librarian says sweetly, passing Jana a pencil and paper. They finish, and JoeJoe tucks Jana's books under his arm, then Greydan leads the way out of the building, back into the crisp fall air.

Standing on the front steps, Jana asks, "Well, guys, do you want to go to my house and make sandwiches or get pizza?" They all agree on pizza and go to Jana's house taking the short route through the lumber yard to get there faster. No one is home, and the doors are locked when they get there, Jana lets them in with the combination. They all know the combo because Mr. Jay told it to them when he installed the lock. Greydan orders the pizza online and asks if they want water or soda to drink before he pays. Jana tells him not to get drinks; there's plenty to drink in the fridge, so they all get something on the way to the playroom. JoeJoe sits on the couch and munches some carrots he had snagged when he got his drink.

Jana asks, "Asa, was there a problem at the library when we were checking out?"

Asa answers, "It was just a weird thought, really. Miss Purty thought she wished she were you. She thinks we're nice-looking and is a little jealous. She has decided you should only have one boyfriend, not all of us. Her idea is that we're indecent. Don't let it bother you, hun. I wouldn't have even told you if you hadn't noticed the face I made while we were there."

No one really knows what makes others feel the way they do, and this group of young people respect the freedom of others to choose. It doesn't really affect any of them, they're used to knowing that there are some who don't like the way they live or what they do. They've made peace with the knowledge and let it go. At least Miss Purty didn't try to hurt them, force her opinion on them, or say her thoughts out loud.

The crew talks through the things they learned at the library. It doesn't take them long to conclude they need more information before they figure out how to help the ones they felt in the mirror. Usually, with Jana's visions, they listen to them and wait for them to happen in real life. Something often happens to show them what the vision is about or leads them straight to the source. Like the Gordon family calling them to clean their home earlier this week. The mirror thing is dangerous, and they need to be ready for this one with as much information as they can gather ahead of time. Not that they're afraid of much, they aren't. They decided long ago that helping others with their gifts is what makes them happy.

It was during this portion of their discussion that Mr. and

Ms. Jay arrive home. They trust the young adults completely and yell hello to everyone before retreating to their own areas of the home.

Jana asks the guys, "Can we plan our joint birthday party for the day after Thanksgiving?"

"Great idea, beautiful, since we'll be out of school for the holiday," says JoeJoe. They just need to check with his and Greyd's parents to see if it's all right. It probably will be, Lucy Sayer loves to plan parties.

The doorbell rings, and Greyd gets up to get the pizza, but Mr. Jay, who's been sitting quietly reading in his study, calls out that he's getting it and will be right there. Jana's mom brings paper plates and drinks for her husband and herself into the playroom with the kids. That they come in with the teens is different but welcome, and the kids smile and make room. Jana's dad brings the pizzas in with a smile and sets them on the coffee table, and everyone digs in.

Mr. Jay says, "Jana, boys, we have something we need to talk to you about." Their attention is changed from planning a party to 'uh oh' in the blink of an eye!

4

A LITTLE NEWS

*T*he quiet in the room is uncomfortable as Mr. Jay begins. The teens shift in their seats, as Jana's dad starts. He's not unaccustomed to speaking to groups. However, with this crew and this news, he seems to struggle a bit more than usual, and he stammers, searching for the words. The kids, after moving to the edge of their seats, stare intently, almost willing the words out of his mouth. Jana holds her breath and stares at her father as he speaks. Asa, the only person in the room who looks relaxed, reaches a hand out to Jana and holds hers in his elegant grasp. She looks to him for a clue, and he gives her a slight nod. No winks or perceptible motion to give away his private message to his girlfriend. Yet, Jana understands and realizes that he's letting her know not to worry. This information her father is about to share isn't harmful or hurtful. It's going to change their lives drastically, though.

Mr. Jay finally leans forward and says, "I know by Christmas time this year, you'll all be eighteen. Not that I think you'll make better or worse decisions than you do now. But you know, you'll be considered adults by the law. You can make certain choices then without trouble from any outside sources or the legal system. Unless you do something illegal … not that I think that'll happen, because I don't." He pauses, obviously frustrated with how this little speech is going. He slaps his hand on his knees. Now Jana and the guys are listening even more intently than before. It's so quiet, you can hear a pin drop on the carpet. With a deep breath, Mr. Jay continues, "What I'm trying to say is, I've accepted a position from my company which will require us to move." Mr. Jay looks at his wife and takes her hand in his. Her smile looks forced, his looks goofy.

The air bursts out of Jana in a loud chuff, and she starts to protest when her dad holds up at hand and says, "Please, let me finish, sweetheart." Mr. Jay finally seems to have a better grip on his short presentation. "The company's buying us a house that your mom and I really like. We've talked about this, little one, and if you want to stay here, we'll let you, and we'll pay the bills until you take them over or make other arrangements. On the other hand, if you would like to move to the city with us, you can. The thing is, we know you. We're sure you will choose to stay with your friends, so we want to give you the option. We're just hoping that if you stay, you take over the bills sooner, rather than later. We're not getting any younger!" Mr. Jay finishes with his typical humorous remark.

Asa gives his girl's hand a little squeeze and releases it as she gets up and gives her dad a hug, "Thank you, dad." Turning and hugging her mom, "Thank you, too, mom. I do want to stay here. It might change one day, but for now, I really want to stay here. At least until I'm on my way to college."

"Well then we have things to plan, and so do you all," says Jerry Jay. He lovingly takes his wife hand in his, and they leave with smiles. Jana's mom, Nichole, turns back and blows her daughter a kiss as they leave and says, "Goodnight, sweetie and you, too, boys."

No sooner had the older Jays left the room, than the teens jump up and begin dancing around the room like when they were kids, hugging each other, laughing, and talking. Don't get the impression that it's been overly challenging for them to be together. With a few exceptions, it hasn't been difficult at all.

All of their parents are okay with their poly relationship. When anyone tried to pry them apart, the perpetrator quickly learned it wasn't going to work. Greyd's dad, Ricky Sayer, was a tough nut. The kids had gone through a rough patch for a few months when he wanted them to conform to his ideal type of family relationship. However, when dropping grades and depression had pulled Greydan out of sports, he changed his mind and decided that he could live with his son being in a relationship with his all of his best friends and his adopted brother. His approval was grudging at first. However, over time, he warmed to the idea to the point that now he acts as if he thought this is how it would be from the beginning.

Jana's parents, Jerry and Nichole, have always been more open-minded about the kids and their relationship. They knew from the start this was special, and the boys take good care of their girl. They know these kids are very different, and together, they find a strength that few ever have in life.

JoeJoe grew up in foster homes and never knew his parents. He found his family in Jana and the others, and they're just what he wants. The big guy was either invisible or abused until the kids bonded, and he'll never want to be without any of them. He lives with Greydan. Actually, what happened was … JoeJoe and Greydan were playing together in the park. Greydan's parents noticed cuts and bruises on JoeJoe's face. After talking with him, they found out he had been beaten up by another kid in the foster home where he stayed. At that, they took him in. He was six years old. The Sayers had dared the foster system to try to take him away. The Director of the New York's ACS, a man named Gary Goyle argued it wouldn't benefit the Administration for Child Services to argue with one of the most influential and affluent families in Duchton. They've been his parents ever since.

JoeJoe calls his friends 'family,' and that's just what they are, and all of them feel the same way. He's very protective of his friends. He's only rivaled in that area by Jana. She may be a little thing, but just try to hurt one of her boys, and she'll kick your ass for a month of Tuesdays. For a while, as a child, JoeJoe wouldn't touch any object and wore gloves regularly. He never told anyone but Jana and the guys why. When he touches items, he 'reads' the history of the object. Reading everything like that can get irritating and personal.

Asa, on the other hand, knows his parents; they're just busy, and he's not with them much. His parents spend most of their time away from home on missionary trips in different parts of the world. They've not been home in months, and even though they love and provide for their son, they see him as independent and able to do for himself. When he was a baby, they would tell people he had, 'an old soul' and 'isn't like others, he likes to be alone.' Asa says, "It's true, that is until I met you guys. Now, you guys are my family."

Kaden's parents are just glad that he was finally able to make friends. They're a typical middle-class American family. His dad, Henry, is a policeman, actually a detective. His mom, Gloria, is a teacher. It was a fear of theirs, when he was little, that he wouldn't have friends or ever marry because of his social awkwardness. Kaden's parents love that he's part of a group of kids who help others. But, they admit, they aren't sure what the little group does, except blessing homes. People in church report that they're good at it, too.

The teens have to go to school in the morning, so they prepare to leave the Jays' house. Greyd pulls Jana to the front door and kisses her lightly, telling her, "I'll see you in the morning. Is there anything you want me to bring you before class?"

She screws up her lovely features before saying, "One of your cook's apricot scones, if there are any made and … you, of course." He kisses her again and moves as JoeJoe walks up to her and puts his hands on her waist.

The big boy lifts her up, and she wraps her legs around his body giggling. He says, "Mí corazón, dress warm tomorrow, the weather says it supposed to snow. I'll see you in class. Pensando en ti." Then JoeJoe leans in and gives her a panty-melting kiss before he moves back and sets her down on wobbly feet. He holds her until she is steady and smiles as he leaves.

When Jana gets back to the playroom. Asa and Kaden have the room all cleaned up from their dinner, and the pizza leftovers are put away. They sit down together on the sofa with Jana in between the boys. She scoots down and puts her legs over Asa's long legs and her head in Kaden's lap and says, "Do you want to stay with me tonight or are you both going home?"

Kaden answers, "I wish, but I have a little homework to finish before tomorrow. I have to go. You stay, Asa, and take care of our girl, will you?" Asa nods at his buddy, and Kaden gets up with Jana and kisses her lightly, then says, "I'll see you tomorrow, sugar. When he's gone, and it's just Asa and Jana, she snuggles into him, he wraps his arms around her, knowing what she's thinking and says, "Yes, I want to stay. Shall we make the bed out or go to your room? Your parents are asleep and won't hear us."

"No, let's stay down here and respect their wishes until they move," she answers out loud, knowing she doesn't have to. The teens have skirted the sex issue for years now. They made a pact that until they're eighteen they will remain virgins and even after, if that's how Jana wants it. She battles her raging hormones more than the boys, and they know she's having a hard time waiting. They give her relief when they're able without going all the way, but it's getting to be more and more of a challenge for all of them, especially when Jana has a particularly clear vision. Her visions are strange in the fact that they leave her in an extra-heightened sexual state.

With the sleeper in the playroom made out, Jana and Asa lay down together. Jana snuggles up to Asa and watches his beautiful face, making him blush. Jana knows he's used to others thinking he is nice looking. With the profession he has chosen, that's a given. He has no modesty and freely shows off his exquisite physique, but when she looks at him this way, he's affected to his very core.

Jana is concentrating intently on what she wants from him, so he can make it happen. He rolls her over softly and kisses her mouth, running his tongue over her lips. With a slight moan, he deepens the kiss. She responds with her body moving under his, resulting in a steel erection within seconds. It's getting so hard to wait, but maybe she can control herself a while longer. Right now, though, she just wants to feel him. With a soft touch, she moves her hand down his hard abs to the hardness of his silky-smooth erection.

He groans lowly in the back of his throat and moves forward in her grasp and whispers, "Hun, I won't be able to hold back, and I'll make a mess if you keep that up." Without words, she reaches for his discarded tee shirt and puts it between them. As high as their hormones are running, neither of them really cares. He slips a finger into her wetness and puts a thumb on her nerve center at the same time. Her breath is coming faster, and he kisses her to swallow any noise she makes as they both orgasm. She falls into his arms beside him, and they both lay there, looking at the ceiling, without a care in the world and a shit-eating grin on both of their faces.

After he catches his breath, he reluctantly pulls his arm from under her and tries to clean himself. She takes the tee shirt from him and wipes his rock-hard abs. After she's finished, she wads the shirt up and throws it beside the bed. "I'll wash it in the morning," she says. Boneless and relaxed, they drift off in each other's arms, satisfied, and confident in each other's feelings.

5

BACK TO SCHOOL

*T*he buzzing of the tardy bell has some students scurrying for their desks at the last minute but not Jana or Kaden, who is in her first-hour with her. The other boys are in another class, but they're together. Mr. McCorckle starts his science lesson by saying, "Class, since this semester is short due to the holidays, I'd like to do something that'll go along with the book but give you plenty of time to complete a more intense learning process. In that regard, I've decided to assign you to complete a storyboard presentation."

From the entire class, "Nooooo. Groan. Ughh." You get the picture; the class doesn't like the idea of being assigned anything to do with a 'more intense learning process.' You'd think he was making them eat liver and onions for a week.

Mr. McCorckle frowns as he raises his hands, palm out to the class. They quiet to listen to the instructions as he writes them on his tablet which displays on the large screen behind him. "You'll have a lot of freedom. You only need to do a study of one of the subjects from chapters one through seven, give facts, present it orally, and in board form. It has to be at least a four-page report and provide an accurate work cited page. Also, Wikipedia had better not be your only resource. Find the source origin of the information. Don't always rely on what someone tells you the information says or means. You can work with a single partner only." There are more groans from the class.

This time, Mr. McCorckle raises his voice to talk over the moaning and groaning. "This will represent seventy percent of your grade this semester. I expect you to put in your best effort!"

Jana and Kaden smile and wink at each other, knowing they will complete this project together. However, before they even finish the wink-smile-wink routine, Mr. McCorkcle pipes up again, "Mr. Walsh, and Miss Jay, you may not partner up again. As my two highest GPA students, I expect you to choose a partner from the others, in fact, Terry Ford will be your partner Miss Jay, and Stacy Perrin will be yours, Mr. Walsh. Looking immensely disappointed, the two friends separate and go over to the specified students to plan their projects. They hope they won't have to complete the entire project alone while the other student rides their coat-tails to receive the same grade which is so frustratingly common these days.

Jana says, "Hi, Terry. How are you? Do you want to sit over here and discuss our project?"

The pimply-faced shy boy looks up and away from her and nods his agreement.

Jana talks to him for a bit, trying to get him to come out of his shell. "You know, Terry, I know you're quiet. I don't mind. But could you open up to me a little? Maybe, we can be friends."

Suddenly, Terry says with a bit more force than is socially acceptable, "I can do the graphics for the board if you want." His sudden outburst catches Jana by surprise, and she stands to stare at him with wide eyes and her mouth agape.

Terry finishes by looking back down at his shoes and saying in a quieter tone, "If you want, I mean if it's okay with you."

Jana, regaining her composure enthusiastically responds with, "No, Terry, you just caught me off guard. I think it's a great idea. I love it."

That was the beginning of Terry opening up with her. After that exchange, Terry seemed much more willing to talk to her. He retains all of his awkwardness, however. But now, he is fully engaged with Jana on the project. They quickly decide on a subject, a title, and exchange cell phone numbers including email addresses, so they can finish faster. Jana is pleased to make a friend of someone so shy. Of course, she wanted her smoldering hunk, Kaden for a partner. That's an impossibility, but she's pleasantly surprised with her assigned partner.

Kaden, on the other hand, spent most of the rest of the class time warding off advances from Stacy. Yes, the very same Stacy who had shamelessly made a play for Greydan the day before. Kaden can barely get her to agree to a subject. After that, she takes over the conversation. "I'll work with you on what you need to write, but I insist that I provide the board and graphics. I know that it could cost a great deal of money. Well, I mean not for me; it wouldn't be much. But ... we all know your parents don't make much. Not that not having money is a problem, of course. You know that I really have to make sure the graphics reflect well on me. As class President and as a cheerleader, I have a reputation. My reputation is on the line and mustn't be tarnished by trashy project tools, even if you are our star baseball pitcher."

With Stacy on her, 'I'm better than you' rant, Kaden isn't able to get any of the little details of the project worked out.

So, when the class bell rings, he all but jumps up and rushes out the door of the science hall to wait for Jana.

When Jana gets out into the hallway with him, she is already laughing at his dilemma. "It'll be okay, and if Stacy gets too out of hand, I'll gladly put her in her place!" Jana's golden-brown eyes are dancing in glee.

"Thanks, sugar," Kaden says. His next class is wood-shop, so he leaves the main building and heads over there, leaving his girlfriend to make her way to her next class. JoeJoe and Asa are there waiting for her, she gladly shares Kaden's discomfort with them by telling them about Stacy.

The rest of the day goes by in a boring school fashion. Afterward, the teens meet in the parking lot, where they decide to go to the diner to get a snack before going home to do homework. While they sit and order drinks, Greyd says, "I talked to my parents and the birthday party is a go for the day after Thanksgiving. I say let's make it a theme party. What about a Riverdale theme, or do you want something more girlie, Jana?"

Jana answers, "Oh, I love the idea. We already have costumes from last year's Halloween to wear. What do you think Asa, Kaden, JoeJoe?" She knows they'll agree to anything she wants, but she likes to be sure. "Looks like we have a theme. Shall we do homework at Greyd's and order invitations?"

The group is talking excitedly about the party when Stacy Perrin struts over to their table. She wants to make sure they look at her. What she doesn't know is they're only looking at her because they can't figure out why she is coming to their table. Greydan has already made his feelings known, and he's preparing to put his foot down when she slips onto Kaden's lap.

In a whiny voice, she asks him, "Will you please come over to my table to work on our project?" She then leans in as if she's about to kiss his cheek when Kaden stands up, still holding her, and places her on her feet. Horrified, he glances at Jana then looks at Stacy and tells her, "Stacy, I've got better things to do than deal with this type of stuff. I may be your partner on this project, but that doesn't make me your boyfriend. Please knock this off." Without waiting on her response, he walks off toward the bathroom.

Jana's temper flares as she stands. "Stacy, he's not interested in you that way. You need to know that he's my boyfriend, and I'm not sharing with you at any time or any place."

Stacy huffs, "Why not, you slut? You're just a creepy trashy girl pretending to be something. You can be replaced. You just watch!" She stomps away feeling satisfied that she'd gotten in the last word.

Jana starts to go after her, not willing to let her get away that easy. Asa quickly, but gently touches her hip, turning her toward him. He shakes his head meaningfully. She understands that he has something he'll tell her later, so she sits back down and lets it go … for now.

Kaden comes back to the table. Looking a little embarrassed, he starts to explain, "Sugar, you're the only girl—" Jana stops him mid-sentence.

"You don't have to explain. I know you love me, and I'm not worried one little bit, handsome. It might not keep me from kicking her ass, but I know you aren't interested in her," Jana explains.

All the boys chuckle as they stand to leave. On the way out, they decide Jana will drive her car home, tell her parents where she's going, then ride with Greyd and JoeJoe to their house. Asa and Kaden will ride in Asa's little black Toyota pickup.

6

THE DRESS

*A*fter dropping off Jana's car, Greyd drives her and JoeJoe to their house where they meet Asa and Kaden, who are already waiting in the kitchen. They grab drinks and open their school books to finish their homework. The teens sit at the granite table with their books open. The Sayer's resident cook, Chela Martinez, is working in the room getting dinner started and making snacks for the kids. She's a little lady, one hundred pounds dripping wet. Her red-blonde hair is pulled into a tight bun and covered by a net. Her green eyes flash as Greydan spills his drink. He quickly grabs a dish towel and has it clean before she makes one of her well-practiced waspish comments. She more than makes up for her diminutive size with her huge personality. No one messes with Chela or the kids she protects and spoils. She'll take you down with one swipe of her sharp tongue and a tug on your ears for extra oomph.

She pulls a sheet of apricot scones from the oven and says, "Jana I made these just for you. I wasn't in a good mood this morning when Greydan asked for them. I didn't have time to make some, so I made them now. You can share with the heathens if you want, it's up to you."

She's still laughing loudly as Lucy Sayer—Greyd and JoeJoe's mother—sashays through the door. She heads straight for her boys and kisses Greyd on top of the head. Even with Greyd sitting, his height is even with her's while she's standing, making for a somewhat humorous picture. Then she tiptoes to reach her other son JoeJoe's forehead causing him to bend down a little where she plants her kiss on his forehead and leaves a little lipstick mark at the same time. Kaden sputters a laugh at his friend, but he recovers quickly, covering his faux-pax with coughs and pounding on his chest as if he'd swallowed his drink wrong. A wry little smile briefly crossing Asa's face is the only acknowledgment from him as he recognizes what Kaden's cough is really about.

Everyone knows JoeJoe is adopted. The Sayers have never hidden it. Everyone also knows he is every bit Lucy's son, and they'd better treat him accordingly.

"I'm so glad you're all here today," she says, "I haven't seen you all in forever. You boys are all so big. I think you've grown six inches since the summer, Kayden. Jana, you're as beautiful as ever. So, do you mind if I interrupt for just a second? I need to ask about the birthday party."

Jana answers for them, munching her scone, "We're just finishing up, anyway, Lucy. We always have time for you."

The kids make sure to call her by her given name. When they were introduced, they made the mistake of calling her 'Mrs. Sayer,' and she sternly corrected them, saying, "I am not old enough to merit a 'Mrs.' title yet."

"What do you need to ask?" Jana continues.

The regal lady says, "I was wondering about a live band or a DJ. I think I can get someone even on this short of notice, but we're having the fall formal and then the Christmas party in December, so I thought that the birthdays should be more of a fun type party. I was thinking of hiring someone to put up some get away rooms." Silence … looking around and seeing the confusion, she continued, "You know those rooms where you get locked in, and you must decipher the pertinent clues to regain your freedom. What do you all think? Too much?"

"Ohhhh," they all say at once, drawing out the word, and trying not to laugh.

"Mom, they're called 'escape rooms,' but yeah, it's a great idea!" Greydan says with a slight grin.

While Greydan is explaining the terminology to his mother, the other teens are animatedly discussing the idea.

"Lucy, we love the idea, and we think a DJ is more our speed," adds Jana.

JoeJoe puts his arm around his mother's shoulder and says, "Mom, we were thinking of making it a Riverdale theme. You know like the 'Archie' comic books?"

"JoeJoe that is a wonderful idea. It's settled then. I'm so glad you like the idea of the getaway rooms, too," says Lucy.

Greydan looks at JoeJoe, and they both laugh and shake their heads without trying to correct their mother. "Also, Jana, I took the liberty of buying you a dress for the fall formal while Jerry and I were in Paris. You don't have to wear it if you don't like it, though, dear. Would you like to see it?"

Jana's breath hitches with excitement written on her face that is as much of an answer as what she says, "Oh, my gosh, yes! You have the best taste, Lucy. I'm sure that I'll love it!" Jana practically leaps from her seat, telling Chela on her way out, "Don't let the boys eat all my scones, please. I'll be back after I try on the dress." The petite blonde Jana is almost squealing with excitement.

Lucy smiles as they shuffle off together. The boys shake their heads, smiling and happy their girl is so pleased.

Jana practically runs up the stairs to the bedroom Lucy has converted to her closet. The elegant Lucy doesn't run up the stairs. Yet, she does get there quickly while still maintaining the stately demeanor she's known for.

When she gets to the room, she opens a long thin white box full of clothing covered in an opulent-looking white and gold tissue paper. Carefully unwrapping the tissue paper Lucy removes a long-sleeved dress … which isn't a dress. This outfit is more of a combination of a tunic and a dress. The design is a modern Asian twist on a Pakistani tunic. The length is floor length in the back and top of the thighs in front, very sexy. It's plum colored with silver flower accents falling down one side and sheer sleeves in black which match a skinny pant emblazoned with the same metallic flower embellishment as the top. Jana can't even talk she is so amazed. Greyd's mom says, "Do you like it, Jana?" She observes the young woman curiously.

"Oh, yes! I absolutely love it," she says in a breathy hum as she runs her fingertips over the delicate material. Tears spill from her eyes, and she turns to hug Lucy. The older woman takes a deep breath and hugs her back, satisfied she did the right thing. She could only have her one son, so she adopted another. But she always wanted a daughter and has been planning all of her life to make friends with the ones that Greydan and JoeJoe chose to be with. She's sure that Jana is the choice for both of her sons and doubts that decision will ever change. But if it does, she decided long ago she is keeping Jana, and the boys will just have to adjust.

Lucy smooths Jana's hair then puts her hands-on Jana's shoulders and moves back a bit to talk to her. "That's not all. I got shoes for you, too. Do you want to try them?"

"Yes, you'd better believe it!" Jana squeaks and claps,

rubbing her hands together. The older female pulls out a pair of silver stilettos, and they get to giggling as Jana puts on her finery. It is almost forty minutes later when she makes it back down to her boys and her scones.

JoeJoe asks, "You aren't going to show us how you look in your new dress, mí corazón?" JoeJoe's dark eyes flash in a romantic smolder.

"No, I'm saving that for the formal," Jana answers secretly thinking of their faces when they see her in her finery.

"We always like to see you, dressed up or not. I'm sure we'll be pleasantly surprised when we do get to see you in the dress. What color is it, so we can match some part of our clothes to you?" Kaden asks.

"Plum, black, and metallic silver, and I can hardly wait to show you all," their girl answers. "Now, I think I want to be Betty for the birthday party. Who are you all going to be?" They're all talking about it when Greydan's dad, Ricky, comes home, and they know it's time to get going. Asa takes Kaden and Jana home, leaving Greydan and JoeJoe to themselves and the Sayers.

On the trip to drop off Kaden, Jana sits in between the boys in the little truck. Her hands rest on their legs; she is rubbing small circles on Kaden when she feels a cold chill and shivers against her boys, telling herself it's nothing. When Asa stops, and Kaden gets out, he leans in and gives her a sly smile with a kiss and tells her he'll see her in the morning. Jana stays close to Asa as he drives off, not wanting to move away from him.

Her Elf Boy says, "I don't know what the shiver means, either, honey, but whatever happens, we will meet it together. We have the best crew ever, and we'll always be there for each other. Are you okay?"

"Yes, I'm okay. I have a bad feeling that something isn't right, nothing specific and no vision, though." She leans her head on his shoulder, suddenly very tired as he pulls up and parks in front of her house and stops.

He gets out, turns, and puts his hands-on Jana's face as he bends toward her and kisses her on the forehead then traces a finger down to her chin. Their eyes lock, and she nods to him, knowing he's telling her how much he cares with his eyes. He lets her out of the door on the drivers' side and pats her butt as she passes him. Walking up to the door, she turns just a little and gives him a flirty wave as she goes in. He watches until she's safe inside before leaving for his own lonely empty house. Maybe he'll ask if he can live with her here after her parents move to the city after the holidays.

7

THE SHIVER EXPLAINED

*I*t's a windy and rainy Friday morning. You know the kind of morning where you want to stay inside, hiding under a blanket, watching some old movies, and drinking hot chocolate all day. It's the kind of a day you really hate, but somedays love. For Asa, though, today seems to hold a foreboding which he can't grasp yet.

Asa's sitting, with Kaden, in his little Toyota pickup truck. Both are lost in their thoughts. Their typical morning conversation washed down the gutters along with the fall leaves, small sticks, and other detritus carried by the fallen rain. Asa waves at Jana as she parks beside him. The wind and rain keep the three of them inside their vehicles until Greydan and JoeJoe arrive. When they get there, they park directly in front of Jana in the student parking lot. Asa waves at Greydan and JoeJoe as they all get out and hurry toward the front doors of the school.

The bustle inside the school seems normal to all of the friends except Asa. To him, the very air is different as if he can smell burnt coffee on a day where he desperately needs the good stuff. Today, something is up. This morning, even the student population at large is acting strangely almost defensive, trying to keep the world at bay.

Asa tugs on Jana and Greydan's arms pulling them off to the side near Jana's locker. There he whispers, "I think there's something wrong."

Jana, looking serious replies, "Yeah, I feel it, too. What is it?"

"Well, at first, the students seemed to be the source. But I figured out they can feel there's a problem. They seem to be just reading the vibe. So, I blocked them and only focused on the teachers. They know what the problem is but are making plans. They are secretive and aren't even thinking of the problem just how to make it easier on us. What I'm sure of is that a girl has been killed. Her body was found outside of town at the truck stop rest area. I haven't heard her name yet. They're planning on telling us in our homerooms. I'll see you at lunch." Asa backs away, ducks his head, and leaves, touching the side of Jana's hand as he goes.

As Jana and Kaden await the coming dreadful news, they take notice of the serious way that Mr. McCorckle is acting this morning. The two have learned that pretending to be surprised along with others is the best way to keep others from mocking them for their gifts. "It's easier to fake our reactions than it is to explain how we knew," Jana has explained several times to the boys. Today, like so many other days, they behave as if they don't know what is going on. Jana joins in on the scuttlebutt … but only to the smallest degree possible. As much as anything, Jana and Kaden sit quietly waiting for the shoe to drop.

The general 'buzz' of the class is different than usual. It seems as if the students are awaiting whatever news that is being so carefully withheld from them for now. Although the collective wisdom is they don't have a clue as to what's happened, the prevailing rumor mill is hard at work coming up with possible explanations, each bit of new gossip more outlandish than its predecessor.

Finally, their science teacher stands and starts, "Students, please sit. I have news that you need to hear this morning. If you're someone who can't handle serious or sad news, I'd like you to make your way to the office and call your parents or guardians. I assure you, you'll still be able to hear the news. However, you'll hear it from your parents or guardian. I must impress upon you the seriousness of what I'm about to discuss. Please don't take my warning lightly. This news might be a trigger." No one leaves after the warning. Now, everyone is waiting, transfixed entirely on every movement or utterance from their teacher.

Mr. McCorckle's tall frame is bent and grim. He nervously clears his throat before he continues, "Early this morning, the sheriff's department issued a curfew of ten o'clock p.m. for anyone under eighteen. I must impress upon you the seriousness of this curfew. The curfew was issued in response to a murder. The body of the victim was found at the East Truck Stop just outside of town. The young woman was killed sometime last night. She was a fellow student. I know what I'm telling you is a shock. He has to stop as the students begin to talk amongst themselves. "Please, listen to me." Mr. McCorckle pauses and raises both hands in the air and pats the air in a calming gesture. After the murmurs quiet, he continues, "The authorities are asking for any information you might have. If you have any information, please notify me, and I'll set a time for you to meet with a representative of the sheriff's department today in the library."

Jana and Kaden are searching the room as are several other students. It's Jana who notices it first … but not by much. "Kaden, where's Stacy?" Kaden doesn't answer, he only looks at Jana with a look of horror on his face. A sinking feeling which matches the shiver and chill from last night in Asa's truck hits the pit of Jana's stomach as she recognizes that Stacy is the dead girl.

Kaden reaches for his girl's hand. He rubs his fingers on her palm as their science teacher continues, "Yesterday, Stacy Perrin was murdered." The room erupts into gasps and cries of 'No,' and 'Oh, God, please no' followed by wretched laments of her closest friends on the cheerleading team.

Mr. McCorckle continues, "The football game for tonight has been canceled along with the pep rally. Please go to study hall instead of the gym during that time. Again, if you have any information pertaining to the crime, please come forward and see me now." A few of their classmates move to the front of the room.

Kaden whispers, "Do you think we should tell him that we saw her after school yesterday, sugar?"

Jana nods, and they both get up together and move forward with the others. Kaden keeps her in front of him with his hand on her waist for support. When they get to Mr. McCorckle's desk they tell him that the information they have may not be essential, but they want to make sure the authorities have it for a timeline if they need it, and they proceed to tell him what they know of the day before.

The teacher writes down their information and says, "I'll tell the deputies. Someone will get back with you if they need to speak to you to get more information. Thank you both, please return to your seats."

After all of the students had a chance to speak to the teacher, he addresses them once again, "You can all work on your projects. Mr. Walsh if you'll work with Ms. Jay and Mr. Ford. Your team will be exempt from the single partner requirement. I'll return shortly. I'm going to give the information you all gave me to the ones in charge. If I'm not back before the end of class, continue with your research at your own pace. When the bell rings, proceed quietly to your next class."

≈

WHEN THE TEENS meet for lunch, the wretched heartache of the student body, as well as that of the staff, is slowly being replaced with a feeling of melancholy expressed as stunned hysteria. Taking in the nervous activity of her peers, Jana says, "I can't believe that Stacy's gone. Even though we weren't friends, we have known her since grade school. You know there's something about the kids you see every day. Sometimes, we know them better than their parents do."

Greyd, looking at Asa, says, "That's true, she was so irritating, but I'd never want this for her. Did anyone learn any of the details of her death yet?"

Asa says very quietly, "The sheriffs are keeping the details confidential. It was a grisly murder, though. I'll tell you more after school. We should meet at Jana's." All the group nods to him before falling back into their own silent contemplation.

Lots of the parents pick up their kids early today. They had heard a few of the details around town and want to be there as a support for their own kids.

Other students speak with the guidance counselors and seem to feel better. On the other hand, Stacy's friends on the cheerleading squad as well as those in student government are almost inconsolable. Many of the football players are with their cheerleader girlfriends, offering a sympathetic shoulder to cry on. Greydan's also been trying to help them today by providing his house for a get-together before curfew. He sends a text to the staff at home and tells them what happened and notifying them that some of the football players and cheerleaders will be there tonight around seven p.m. for a couple of hours just for support and a sort of wake for Stacy. He gets a return text from the house steward that they will have added security tonight at the house.

Being that they are so young, they are in limbo. Waiting to know what to do is hard on them; when they meet in the parking lot after school, the stress is showing. JoeJoe rides home with Jana in her Honda Fit. None of the guys want her to be alone right now, not even on a short ride from school to home. At least not until they're sure the danger is passed.

8

WHAT HAPPENED

*J*ana parks in her usual spot in front of the house, and Asa pulls up close behind her. The others park on the other side of the street and walk over. Their trip to the playroom is more like a procession of monks into a 16th-century monastery instead of into their preferred area. They stop by the fridge and get drinks and snacks before sitting in the playroom, waiting on Asa to begin his briefing of his telepathic theft of knowledge regarding Stacey's murder.

Like the rest of the room, Asa's eyes are sad as he begins, "Guys, you can't tell anyone what I'm about to say because only the police know all of what I'm about to share. If this gets out, you and most likely the rest of us will be accused of being part of her murder." Asa emphasizes the word 'will' and pauses for effect, catching each of his friend's gazes before he moves on.

"Stacy was beaten and killed in the woods then dragged to the truck stop behind the restrooms. Her killer didn't bother to pose her, but did throw trash on her body to hide it. Her class ring and thumb ring are missing. Her school bags were found at the diner where we saw her yesterday. Several students reported they saw her sitting in Kaden's lap, too. Something else, Collin Grimes was with her after we left her at the diner, and he's feeling very guilty because they fought over her sitting in Kaden's lap. The last he saw of her, she was stomping out of the diner and walking toward the parking lot. Collin hasn't told anyone about this yet."

The shaking starts in Jana's hands and quickly moves to her entire body. From the onset of the shaking to the beginning of her vision is less than a few seconds. As she enters her vision, a thick smoky haze replaces the room, even though her eyes are still wide open. This fog is usually where she is before she begins to see any part of her vision clearly. Soon, she begins to visualize the events of yesterday's late afternoon. As she does, she slides off of the couch onto the floor before any of the guys can catch her. JoeJoe picks her up in a flash cradling her to his chest with his arms under hers and locked around her stomach.

He blurts, "She's breathing fine," JoeJoe knows that he only needs to hold her tight enough that she doesn't fall and hurt herself, but he clutches her close, anyway.

Asa adds, "I don't see any cuts or scratches."

Jana moans and says, "I don't think so, freak." It isn't Asa she's talking to. In her vision, she sees a gloved set of hands beating Stacy. Jana's trying to get the guy to notice her and stop hurting Stacy. Jana's on the outside of the vision looking in, when the figure looks up, reacting to some noise or something. Jana sees his face clearly. She knows this man. He's one of the homeless men she's seen around town and begging in the park. The murderer sets back to his task of killing Stacy as if someone just reminded him he had an unfinished job. After completing his gruesome task, he methodically steals her purse and the rings off of her hands. The vision ends. Everyone has seen this guy around.

The clairvoyant teen is starting to feel her body again and is very aware of JoeJoe as he holds her close. Her core flames at the thought of him pressed against her, and she climbs up his frame and presses her wetness to him. Feeling him harden under her she starts to move on him then feels someone at her back; it's Greydan, she can tell because he smells like soap and spice. Her back arches into him enjoying the feel of two of her guys when she hears Greyd say, "Fuck, Jana, you're going to kill me. It's not the right time yet. I promise you, it'll be here soon, though, and we'll take care of all of your needs."

JoeJoe tells his girl that what Greydan says is right, and they have to wait a little while longer.

Asa is moaning, "Shit, you guys are making me hard enough to cut diamonds. Please, think of something else."

Jana is coming around and is more aware, relaxing with a smile. Opening her golden eyes, she gazes into JoeJoe's black depths and kisses him full on and deeply. His groan brings her fully back to reality, and she slides down his body.

"Not helping, honey," Asa murmurs.

"I know who did it, guys. It's the homeless guy that we see in the park. We saw him last week. He's the creepy one who was begging for work at the diner and then wouldn't take it when Mr. Smith at the drugstore tried to get him to sweep around the store and the curb." They all remember him.

"What do we do?" Greydan asks, "We can't just tell the sheriff's department, they'll think we did it. Even though we have a name in town for our gifts, the town people really don't have a clue about what we can do."

Kaden answers, "I've got an idea. My dad just made detective this year. We could tell him … if you want."

The teens like that idea, they sit and brainstorm ways to

tell Detective Walsh, so he'll believe them. They all play devil's advocate with each one shooting down each idea, one at a time. That is each of them except talking to Kaden's dad in private and proving what their gifts are. Then they just have to hope he believes them.

Kaden says, "I'll set up the meeting tonight, and I'll let you know."

That's when Jerry and Nichole come home and rush into the playroom and hug all the kids, telling them how glad they are that they're safe. … A text is just not enough.

Jana explains, "Mom, dad, we have a get together for the football team and cheerleaders at Greyd's, but I promise I'll be back before curfew." She assures them that the Sayers have added extra security, and they will all be safe.

Sighing, Nichole Jay says, "That's a very thoughtful thing for you to do. I appreciate you taking care of others, but please be vigilant and take care of yourselves. I don't want any of you alone. Asa, you'll be staying here until the murderer is caught. I'm sure your parents will agree with me. Jerry, it looks like we're on our own tonight. It seems that our daughter has plans."

He nods to the teens and chuckles, taking his wife in his hands from behind and tells her, "I'd love to take you out, love, but I'm almost afraid to leave with you. How about I call for delivery?" Then he adds, "And, boys, don't let Jana out of your sight," pointing at each one of them in turn.

The boys all agree that at least one of them will be with her at all times. Mr. Jay nods to them and says, "Okay, then you can go, Jana. I need some time alone with your mom, anyway."

"Okay … you two need a room," Jana jokes with her parents. All the boys and Jana stand and grab their coats and gloves as they move toward the door to leave.

Greyd puts on a knit cap and says, "I'll make sure your

daughter's home by nine thirty p.m., and I'll also make sure that Asa is either with her or that he stays with us."

The kids walk out the door as the Jays tell him, "Thank you!"

9

A WAKE OF SORTS

*T*he cold November sun had set at least an hour earlier as Jana Jay and her crew of boys reach the Sayer house. Wow! They weren't kidding when they said they were adding extra security tonight. While she waits at the gate, a live guard stands ready to check IDs and to enter the access code needed for guests entering the Sayer complex. The guard is someone that Jana and the other boys know well.

Jack Dewey has been working for the Sayers for years and waves the teens in after punching in the code and opening the gate for them. They wave at him as they drive through. That is everyone except Asa waves. Asa seems to have had his fill of being social for the day.

Jana notices his social slight and decides that Asa's been overstimulated today. She knows the shock of reading the murder and the effect it had on all those in the school today would take its toll on anyone. On her kind-hearted Asa, it must have been grueling. *Asa will need some alone time soon. Maybe tonight when we get home, we can lay down and stare at the stars through the skylight in the playroom until we drift off to sleep. I'll talk to the guys, and maybe we can tone down the activity on Sunday, so he can have a little peace.* She always looks after her boys, trying to find ways to make them happy and take care of them.

As Jana leads her group through the front door, she notices that Lucy Sayer and her staff have decorated to support a soothing quality in the room. The generous seating, calming music, and even the lighting is all to set a calming and reflective tone for the teenage guests.

With Jana in the lead, they enter the ballroom. This large room has hosted some of the most extravagant social events in the region. Lucy Sayer is well known for her skill as a hostess. The walls of this room have seen lavish galas and glamorous charity banquets. There is room enough for swirling dresses and strutting tuxedos, musical and vocal performances, as well as the dinner tables to seat at least seven score.

Tonight though, there will be less than fifty guests; almost double if you count the staff and additional security. Jana pauses to take in the complexity of the decorations. The large room seems intimate. A projector screen is displaying a remembrance video and a 'how to handle grief' message.' At the end of the room where they normally have the band, are tables of food and drinks. Everything is finger food, it's lovely and exceedingly tasteful.

Jana turns to Greydan and JoeJoe and says, "Greyd if you and JoeJoe would like to go change and clean up, I'll stay here and greet anyone who comes in. Kaden, do you mind staying with me? I'll feel better just knowing you're here. Asa, someone needs to talk to security and help them verify the kids that are coming here tonight. That'll get you a little bit of peace and away from the crowds for a while. Is that okay? Am I too bossy?"

"It's just perfect, baby, see you in a few minutes," Greyd

says, bending to kiss Jana lightly before moving out of the way for JoeJoe to give her a quick kiss, too. Asa follows Greyd and JoeJoe to the second floor before leaving them to find the security room to help verify their fellow students.

It takes just a few minutes before the first of the football players begin to filter into the party room. Jana stands near the entrance and greets them with hugs and expressions of sympathy as Kaden shadows near her. He nods and pats his friends on the shoulder when it's called for, but mainly, he just stands behind his girl.

When the cheer squad begins to filter in, they're inconsolable. This is where Kaden's gift of manipulation fits in so well. He's able to use his voice to get people to do what he wants. His close friends have never seen him fail … if he wants something bad enough. He's not the type to abuse his gift, and his crew knows this. They trust him.

His hand is low on Jana's back as he moves forward to the weeping cheer squad. Kaden deepens his voice and speaks in a slow melodic pattern. Generally, this has the intended effect of turning Jana's knees into butter and setting her panties on fire. This time, he has it turned down a bit and has it directed at the sobbing cheerleaders.

Kaden says, "Don't cry, Angel," he tilts the chin of one of the more disconsolate cheerleaders upward. "Stacy's always going to be part of us." He moves his warm hands to the shoulders of another. "As long as you remember her, she will not be forgotten." Now he takes in hand two cheerleaders, and while looking back and forth into their faces, continues, "Remember how blessed you were to have her in your life. Remember the fun things she did to make your life better?" He steps back letting his hands rest upon the shoulder of two other girls. "Maybe think of being able to be her friend as a blessing not a bad thing, because she's gone."

The effect isn't sensual, but Jana knows from experience

he could have made it that way. It is just enough to get the girls off of their path of misery and back onto the joy that Stacy had brought into their lives. Both Kaden and Jana give hugs to the girls to show their friends to seats. They've all stopped crying and moved on to talk about funny things that Stacy had done or how talented a gymnast she was.

Jana looks at Kaden and gives him a conspiratorial wink. He gratefully returns her smile, winks, and puts his arm behind her, resting his hand at her lower back. With the two largest groups out of the way, Kaden and Jana continue greeting and consoling the rest of the kids who have come to the wake … of sorts. Jana happily welcomes the guests and lets Kaden continue with his positive message. The kids who hear it are happy to listen and to take his advice.

Greydan and JoeJoe are working the room like a couple of professional marketers. They have cleaned up and returned to visit with their friends. They are urging everyone who came, to eat and drink something. When JoeJoe finds someone too shy to get their own, he gets them something. Jana watches him from the doorway. His large frame might have some people wary, but she appreciates the ripple of his muscles as he moves. He catches her staring at him and smirks at her in return.

She's happy and glances around to find Greyd again thinking to steal an admiring peek. When she finds him, he's apparently sick. He's sitting with his head held between his hands staring at the floor. She gives an eye to Kaden who moves with her to Greyd, hoping to help. Most of the students who were coming are already here. Others can greet the few friends left to arrive.

Jana reaches her boy and asks, "Greyd, is something wrong?"

He looks up, his blond hair falling into his eyes, his chiseled features full of pain, and gives her a slight nod. His beautiful blue eyes look hauntingly into hers as he tells her, "Stacy's spirit is here and standing on the stage as we speak. I don't want to worry you, but she's walking around trying to get people to talk to her. I don't think she knows she's dead."

Jana puts her hand on his face to comfort him and says, "I'm here for you. We can help."

Kaden asks his buddy, "Tell me where or walk me to her, and I'll tell her. I know it is hard for you because you can see them. Greyd, we're a team. I don't mind talking to her. Jana, do you mind going to get Asa, so we know what she's saying or thinking?"

Jana shakes her head and hurries away. In a moment, she's back with Asa, and they walk up to the others on the stage. Greyd ushers them to the spot they need to be to speak to Stacy. He clearly sees the spirit, and she notices that he sees her and makes motions with her hands, trying to talk to him. The area of the room where she stands is much colder than the other areas of the room. Jana and her guys have goosebumps.

Asa asks, "Can any of you hear her?" They all shake their heads no, so he continues. "She's saying she's sorry for how she treated you, Greydan and Kaden. That she was in the park, and she doesn't understand how she got here. Kaden, …"

Kaden moves in front of Asa where he gently asks Stacy's spirit, "Please follow us to the sound stage." He points at the room next to the stage. He says, "We'd like to speak with you in private."

The real reason is they don't want the others in the room to notice them talking to thin air since most people obviously can't see the ghost of their friend. Stacy agrees, so Kaden takes the lead and walks quickly to the sound room. While the little room is nearby, its best assets is it offers them the useful ability to see out, while not allowing others to see them.

Greydan says, "She's here with us." And he shuts the door behind himself. He continues, "She looks scared, and I'm guessing she already knows what's happened to her.

Asa adds, "Greyd is right. She's afraid, but she needs to know for sure that she's passed.

Kaden speaks slowly, and he lowers his voice an octave, "Stacy, it's okay that you flirted with us. We don't hold that against you. None of us do." He pauses and looks around the room, stopping at Jana. All of their heads are nodding in agreement. "Do you believe us, Stacy?"

Asa tells the crew, "She's crying a little, but her voice is steady. She's glad that we're not angry. She wants us to know she thanks us for not holding a grudge against her." Asa looks back to Kaden and gives a silent nod for him to continue.

"Stacy, you need to know something. It isn't horrible. It's just a new reality for you. That day in the park … you were killed. This get together is a sort of wake to help your friends accept your death and prepare their goodbyes for you. Stacy, can you understand me? Do you need some time to think?"

Asa answers for Stacy, "She's telling me that she's afraid she had been killed. Does anyone know who killed her? Because she needs that asswipe caught!"

They all chuckle a little at her swipe of anger at her killer.

"Stacy is laughing at her joke with us. She thinks she may have to stay here until her murderer is in jail. Maybe then she'll be able to move on. Someone or something told her this is the case, but she doesn't remember for sure. She wants to know if we'll help her?"

Greydan says, "Yes, of course, we will help. We're just figuring out how to do that very thing. It might take us a few more days so that we're not accused because we know too much about the crime. Jana saw the homeless guy who killed you. So, we know who did it. How is it that you were with him anyway, Stacy?"

The ghost tells them, through Asa, her whole story. That she was feeling like no boys would ever like her after she hit on Greydan and Kaden, and they didn't want her. Then she had a fight with Collin, the only boy who had shown her any interest. He was upset that she had sat on Kaden's lap at the diner. He was interested in her, and she didn't even realize it.

She says she was having a pity party and trying to figure out how to make it up to Collin when the homeless guy told her that he needed help. He said there was a kitten stuck in a ditch, and he couldn't rescue it because he's too old to climb anymore. She wanted to help and went with him to help save the kitten. The old man pointed to where the kitten was, and when she looked, that's when he hit her with a club over and over … until …

Kaden stops her, "That's enough information, Stacy. We understand … you don't need to relive it."

Asa told them she agreed. Then Greydan says, "She just faded out and isn't here now.

Jana quietly says, "Well, guys, it looks like we need to help her move on. Do we all agree?" They were more upbeat than they'd been all day as they agreed with Jana.

Kaden says, "I'll call you all tomorrow after I talk to my dad. If I get to tonight, I'll text you tonight, the sooner, the better." After more head nods around the room, he holds open the door, and they go back into the party room.

The students are doing better, and there's even some laughter as they tell stories of how Stacy would joke with them and do this fake falling shtick during the football games to make the crowd laugh. Most of the players had seen it on social media, but none had seen her do it live.

Jana notices Collin in the corner, so she and her boys go to console him. Once again, Kaden takes the lead to help

Collin understand that those who have passed on don't usually hold grudges against the living. Especially those who were cared for like Stacy did for him. "Collin, we knew Stacy liked you. She would never hold a grudge against you. You also didn't cause this, and even if you hadn't fought, you couldn't have prevented it." Collin is still a little down on himself, but his spirits pick up some.

At nine-twenty pm, Greydan announces, "If you want to meet curfew, it's time to leave."

Mrs. Jay interjects, "You are more than welcome to have another get together here if needed. We would be most happy to see you all again."

"Thank you's" to Mr. and Mrs. Jay, along with more hugs and shoulder patting, accompanied by some tears, and still more smiles are offered as the students all file out the door to their cars. Security observes them, making sure nobody is trying to walk away from the wake.

Jana places a hand on Greyd's chest and says, "You're amazing for thinking of this and helping so many of the people we see almost every day cope with this tragedy."

She rises onto her tiptoes to kiss him goodnight … he has to bend a little for her to reach. Then Jana reaches for her gentle giant JoeJoe, who also has to bend for her to kiss. The crew says their goodbyes, and before Asa, Kaden, and Jana leave, she gives tight hugs to the Sayers. Then taking one of each of their hands says, "Thank you for letting us use your home and providing all of the food, drinks, security, and all of the other things you did to pull this off so fast. You two are amazing people."

"You are so welcome, dear. But this is what we do in life, we help people."

Jana loves that about the Sayers. They say it, and they mean it.

10

A LITTLE ALONE TIME

*J*t is getting a bit colder out; a storm is brewing when Kaden gets out of Asa's truck. He exits, and Asa yells, "Be safe, bro, and try to stay out of trouble."

Kaden answers chucking, "Who me? You're the one who needs to stay out of trouble!" He turns to Jana, "Night, sugar." He kisses his girl. She takes a deep breath and enjoys the fresh smell of him turning her insides to jelly before he takes off racing to his house. *Damn, that guy is hot!*

Asa laughs and says, "He doesn't have a butt!" before adding, "on any other night I'd take you for hot chocolate and dessert, but we'll be late if we do. I also really need some quiet time. I'll take you for breakfast tomorrow if you want, though. What do you say, pretty girl?"

"I love the idea, and I love spending time alone with you. I can make us hot chocolate, and we have cheesecake in the fridge," Jana says then asks, "Elf Boy, does it feel weird to talk to the dead, or is it the same as with the living?"

"It does feel different, I'll try to explain it. It's like eating cheesecake without smelling it. Does that make any sense?"

"Yes, it does. I just wonder if it hurts you. Because I don't want you to do it if it does. We'll think of another way if we need to."

"No, it doesn't hurt," he says as they ease to a stop in front of the Jays' home. After he has the truck in neutral and the parking brake set, he turns it off before he opens the door and waits for Jana to get out on his side. They are holding hands as they walk toward the front door of the house. Jana steps onto a raised part of the sidewalk and slips. Asa, always vigilant, is there. Scooping her up, he carries her the rest of the way to the door. He might not be as big as the other boys, but he's powerful. Not that it's really needed for Jana! She's just under a hundred pounds of mostly muscle, which isn't a challenge to any of her boys.

He puts her down and holds her steady then opens the door. They take off their shoes and coats. As Asa hangs his and Jana's coats, she goes to the kitchen to make their hot drinks. Asa waits in the playroom for her. She gets the cheesecake from the fridge and cuts a few heart shapes from some leftover fondant for Asa's piece. Then she drops some marshmallows in his cocoa trying to form a heart with little success. When she's finished, she brings a large mug of his drink and his hastily decorated cheesecake to her handsome boy. "I'll be right back, Elf Boy."

While she's in the kitchen, her parents come home and greet her. She pours them a cup of hot chocolate, too, then adds their marshmallows.

"Thank you, princess. Goodnight," her father, says.

"Thank you, baby. We'll see you in the morning." Her mother kisses her on the cheek then chases after her husband. "Jerry Jay, you didn't take your shoes off, and you tracked snow in! And dear, you left your coat out. You married a wife, not a maid."

"There could be room for both. Hey, where's that sexy maid outfit I bought you?"

Jana laughs. Her parents love each other deeply. But they love teasing each other just as much.

Asa is leaning back on the couch when she walks back into the playroom. His girl stops to admire him, beginning with his long sexy legs stretched out in front of him. Her eyes journey to his groin, pausing just long enough for her sexy thoughts to entice an erection. Since he's already shirtless, she gazes at his toned abdomen. Finally, she shifts her gaze to his arms. Asa knows Jana loves his biceps, so he accentuates them by tucking his hands behind his head as he lounges. He won't admit this is anything other than an innocent positioning of his body. Subtly, or most likely not so subtly, this position flexes his biceps in a way that will arouse his girlfriend. A smile breaks out on his face as he realizes he has the desired effect on her.

Jana smiles, too, "I know you can hear what I'm thinking. I'm sure one lucky girl, Asa. You're fine."

They laugh and flirt with each other as they drink their hot chocolate and finish their dessert. Asa needs time to let his mind unwind from all the voices invading his thoughts over the last day. Jana makes sure all he has to think about is her.

With their dessert finished, they move the sleeper sofa under the skylight, so they can watch the stars and talk to each other. Unfortunately, it's just beginning to rain, blocking any stars they might have otherwise been able to see. The light tic-tic sound is soon followed by the heavier drumming as the rain bounces off of the canopy of the skylight. These sounds combine with the gurgling of the water rushing from the gutters to form a calming symphony for both teens. She's resting her head on his chest, listening to the sound of his heartbeat adding to the meteorological opera playing on the roof.

The sound of silence overtakes them, and they fall fast

asleep, neither wanting to disturb the other, both succumbing to the therapy provided by the rain.

The next morning, Jana carefully tries to extricate herself from Asa's arms without waking him. She fails. Asa opens his crystal-green eyes and says, "Good morning, honey."

She turns toward him with a start and falls into the energy of his glance. It's irresistible. Unable to look away, she playfully answers, "Good morning, Elf Boy." Then, she reminds him that he promised her breakfast, "I want raspberry French toast from Maize's just up the street."

"Well, get up and get dressed, and I'll take you," Asa says, grinning, "Text the others. Find out if they want to meet us there. I'm going to get a quick shower in the downstairs bathroom."

She jumps up, runs upstairs to get ready herself, and texts the others, then tells her parents her plans, saying, "Mom, dad I'll be out most of the day with the boys."

Mr. Jay firmly replies, "Miss Jana Jay, you stay with them at all times. No running off by yourself, even for a short time. Do you understand?"

"Yes, dad, I promise I'll stay with one of them, and I'll stay alert." Jana manages to speak to her parents in a polite, even charitable way. After all, she's due to be eighteen in a few days. That means she's an adult. Right?

When Jana and Asa enter Maize's Restaurant, they see that Greyd and JoeJoe already have a table and motion them over. Jana points at her friends letting the Maître d' know where their friends are seated. Although, for Maize's calling Carol a Maître d' is a little like calling the playground merry-go-round a theme park carousel. Carol runs the coffee bar at Maize's when Maize herself isn't here. Which, given that she's seventy-eight, is more than it used to be, but much more than it should be... according to her doctor anyway. If you were to ask her about it, she would tell you,

"That doctor needs to mind his own business, and I'll mind mine!"

Sitting beside Greyd, Jana remembers a scene, like a déjà vu moment, only it's not a replay of something that's happening now. The feeling's the same to her, though. "Guys, listen to this."

All three of her boys stop and immediately focus on what she's saying. They know her well enough to know she'd only interrupt if it were important.

"I just had a déjà vu moment. I saw us sitting around a table, laughing and talking. Then a homeless person walks up and tells us to back off. That's crazy, right?" She adds a laugh, knowing her boys will understand the laugh is just protective coloration for her story. Making it sound funny in case they need to play it off as a joke.

"Yeah, but what's it mean?" Greyd asks. They all look at each other puzzled.

A few seconds later, Kaden walks over and sits next to Jana. She repeats what she saw, reiterating it's déjà vu for any prying ears. Kaden looks at her and shrugs.

Their waitress takes their drink orders and returns with them in short order, asking if they're ready to order. They're all such creatures of habit, they all order the same things every time they're here. They laugh with the waitress at their own predictability, and the waitress turns, leaving for the kitchen with a smile on her face.

After stuffing themselves, Kaden says, "I talked to my dad. He has today off and would talk to us at ten o'clock. If that's okay with you guys." Kaden is careful to not say any secrets out loud. They learned a long time ago that being at your own table doesn't make a privacy bubble around them.

Each of them clearly remembers the encounter back when they were in the sixth grade. Their parents were letting them spend Jana's birthday dinner together and dropped them off at the Forni's Pasta Emporium. They had a wonderful time without their parents for the first time. They were enjoying the moment so much they didn't monitor their conversation. They were laughing and joking about a spirit Greydan had seen who wanted help to cross into the other world. The funny part is, this spirit wanted a kiss from Jana first. The boys teased her and never noticed that Mr. and Mrs. Lopez from the downtown church were at the next table listening to them.

They thought everything was fine until the next day. That's the day that the proverbial solid excretory product, evacuated from the bowels, hit the fan. Mr. Lopez had a talk with Kaden's dad, officer Walsh, at the time at work, saying, "Those kids need to be watched better because they were in public making wild speeches about talking to ghosts as if they're real!" He added, "That girl in the group had her eyes on more than just your son. That's sinful behavior, and you should make sure that wanton behavior is dealt with before it gets out of hand … like their lies about ghosts. In fact, those kids probably need to see Father Bastian at confessional before they stray too far into their crazy made-up worlds."

After arriving home from school, they'd each had to explain to their parents about the incident. Jana's experience was the easiest time. She was able to tell her parents the truth, and they understood. They cautioned her that, ethically, to keep a secret, you didn't speak about it in public. They also made her do a research paper on what the world does to any Frankenstein.

Greydan and JoeJoe could only tell half-truths to their parents. They were both grounded.

Kaden just stood there and took a verbal spanking from his dad on proper public behavior. He never touched the subjects of Jana or ghosts with them again.

Asa's parents were interested and wanted to know more. They started teaching him what they knew of the supernatural.

Needless to say, they had it worse in school, too. They had the typical taunts from the students that none of the teachers or administrators were ever able to hear. It turns out that the message had reached the school, and they certainly didn't want to have to deal with any irate parents crying about "Little Johnny failed his test because those kids placed some sort of hex on him." Eventually, it all blew over, but the crew learned a valuable lesson. Never, ever speak frankly about their abilities in public again ... especially in a restaurant.

Speaking with Kaden's dad will be another learning experience. They'll be meeting him in about an hour at his home. When they do, they'll try, for the first time, to convince someone they have supernatural gifts. Not only that they have the gifts, but they use them to help people in the town, and they even help ghosts. As always, they'll brave it together.

Today, they need Detective Walsh's help. Good thing it will be Kaden who's the one leading the conversation, convincing his dad their gifts are real. He will also have to be the one to help his dad understand that they know who killed Stacy ... all this while making sure he believes them when they say they had nothing to do with the murder of Stacy Perrin.

"Remember we're meeting at Kaden's house at five 'til ten. That'll give us time to grab a drink before we meet with Mr. Walsh," Greyd reminds everyone, "don't worry, we got this," he adds. That's easier said than done.

11

CONFIDING IS HARD

*J*ana and Asa are the last to arrive at the Walsh residence. Jana laughs and shares a giggle, "This looks more like a used car lot than a house!"

Asa laughs nervously with her. She knows he's nervous after what he's had to deal with over the last few days and can't blame him.

The crew, less Kaden, gather at the front door of the Walsh house. Jana pauses to take a few seconds ... for Asa really. One last gasp of peace before he's hit with the thoughts of others. He's been this way all of his life, so it is natural, but sometimes it gets intense, and he needs quiet time ... like yesterday. It's one of the reasons he doesn't talk to many people besides his best friends and Jana. He knows what they're thinking, anyway, and it wouldn't be like him to try and change what they believe.

He nods to his girl, and she rings the doorbell. Kaden's sister Tina answers the door and tells them to come in and that the others are in her dad's office waiting. Asa shifts behind Jana and away from Tina. That usually indicates he's protecting himself. Jana wants to ask him, but that will have to wait. She just smiles at Tina and lets her lead the way.

Mr. Walsh stands and waves them in saying, "Hi, kids, come on in and have a seat, so we can talk. I see you have something to drink, but if you want anything else just let me know, okay?"

Jana looks to Kaden, and he starts, "Dad, we have something to share with you that will think is pretty strange. We're ready to show you proof if you need it. I'm guessing you will, just hear me out, please. We need your help with a problem."

Mr. Walsh's visage turns serious. He puts on his detective's face and motions for Kaden to continue.

Kaden takes a sip of his drink, then a deep breath, "Dad, we know who killed Stacy Perrin, and ..."

Mr. Walsh's face reddens as he all but shouts, "What the fuck, young man? This isn't something I'm at liberty to discuss with you. If you have information about the case, why didn't you give it to the Sheriff's Department when they were at your school on Friday?"

Jana goes for it, to take the heat off of her boy, "Mr. Walsh, he's telling the truth. We can't just tell anyone, sir, because of the way we know. Please, let me continue, all of us have what we like to call special gifts. They're paranormal in nature." The young clairvoyant notices his look of disdain but plows ahead before he can scoff aloud. "In fact, if you think of a number right now Asa will tell it to you ... any number at all."

Asa says, "You're thinking $5,578.31 That is what you owe on your car note, and you are thinking two now and changing it to 247."

Mr. Walsh says, "Wow that is some trick, young man what if I write a number? Can you tell me that?" Kaden's dad writes a number shielding it from all the teens in his office.

Asa tells him, "You wrote 999 but are thinking 1,756,523. You are also wondering if we are all able to tell what you are thinking and worry that I might find out ... private things."

Mr. Walsh nods his head and says, "All true, I'm sure that you all know that young Asa is correct. What do each of you do, if I might ask, now that I'm almost a believer?"

This is when Kaden takes back over and tells him each of their gift including his. Then he explains how they know how Stacy died. Mr. Walsh is sitting back in his chair, steepling his fingers and nodding his head when his son finishes with every relevant piece of information. The last thing that Kaden tells him is, "All of us have agreed to show you what we do if you need to see it in action. All except for Jana because of the way it affects her." They all try to hide Jana's gift because of the sexual heat which overcomes her after her vision is over. However, right now, she's already had the vision, so there's no problem with merely telling Mr. Walsh what she saw concerning Stacy's death. After they finish all of the explanations of their gifts and provide Mr. Walsh the information they have, they sit in silence and wait.

Jana's heart is racing. Not because of the closely held secrets they had disclosed, but more because they were revealed to Mr. Walsh. The guy who, a few years ago, verbally spanked Kaden. The man who told the other parents things that wound up getting them all in trouble.

Jana is preparing more arguments and trying to think of anything more persuasive than what they've said when the detective speaks, "Now I understand why you've all been so close all these years. I believe you. We've used clairvoyants and other paranormal experts to solve cases for us with varying degrees of success. I will say that there've been cases which we could only have solved with their help. The problem is, I'm not the detective on this case, and it's not even in the Police Department's jurisdiction. The crime happened outside of the city limits and is being investigated by the Sheriff's Department. I can talk to the DA and submit evidence or say that I have a confidential informant who gave me information concerning the case. I might advise them that I've had success with a clairvoyant in the past if you would be able to act in that capacity, Jana. However, I'd like for you to perform the exercise as if you were just getting the information and work with a special officer to create a sketch of the possible perpetrator. Will you do this, and are you eighteen yet? Are any of you eighteen? I know Kaden will be by the end of the month."

JoeJoe answers, "I'm eighteen as of September twenty-fourth sir. Jana's birthday is tomorrow, and the rest of us will be eighteen this month with Greydan turning eighteen at the end of December."

Mr. Walsh responds, "Good to know. JoeJoe since you're eighteen you'll be my informant. I'm hoping your age will let you carry more weight than someone younger. Jana, you'll be able to be used as a clairvoyant advisory to the case. I'll have to get back with you sometime tomorrow after I talk to the DA. Will you all be able to help me in the future, if I need you?" All the crew of teenagers nod their heads and respond with a group, "Yes, sir!" as they get up to leave.

Before they get out the door, though, Mr. Walsh tells them, "Thank you for telling me the truth. I believe the five of you are amazing young people." His eyes seemed shinier than usual as his gaze pauses on Kaden. He turns away before Jana can see anything. He can't hide it from Asa who tells everyone how grateful Kaden's dad is to finally know the truth.

Jana has to pee so takes leave of the boys. She turns the corner in the hallway and almost runs straight into Tina as she is heading from her room toward the living room where the boys are. Jana knows the boys are a magnet for girls and hasn't ever noticed Tina act interested in any of them before but feels a shot of jealousy. Still, with Mother Nature yelling at her, she proceeds on to the restroom.

Jana's been avoiding mirrors since she had the mirror vision. As she enters this bathroom, she realizes it isn't possible. The restroom has a double sink with a mirror covering the entire wall above the sinks. The wall behind the sinks has a floor to ceiling mirror. Jana avoids anything more than a quick glance toward the mirror until she washes her hands. As she lets the warm water run over her hands, she looks up into the mirror. She jumps back, stifling a squeal as she sees a figure in the mirror behind her. She squares her shoulders and forces herself to look again, this time for information. Nothing is there. Not one to believe in coincidence, she files the event away for later.

Something smells fantastic when she gets back to the boys who are now sitting in the Walsh's large family-sized kitchen eating the cookies that Mrs. Walsh set out for them. Tina is sitting close to Greydan, obviously flirting with him. She is pretty and must have known they were coming over because she dressed to get attention. Greyd is politely ignoring her. Jana pauses at the door, mentally laughing at Greyd's predicament. She notices how hard he's working at not paying Tina any attention.

Jana walks in the room, and Greydan eyeballs her with relief. He scoots over and lets Jana sit in his chair by Tina. She jumps up in a perfect display of teenage attitude and departs the room in a huff.

"Well, what are we doing for the rest of the day, guys? Kaden and I have a project to work on, but it's not due for a couple of weeks. Is everyone caught up on your homework?" Jana asks deflecting to a new subject.

They all say they are.

Greydan asks, "How about we go to the skate park and have some fun?" That's a perfect suggestion from Greydan, who has paid for them all to have season tickets at the ice rink and wants them to use them.

12

ATHLETES EVERYONE

*H*aving fun together is typical for the crew of teens, but today is especially fun. They love skating and are excellent athletes. They have been skating together since the rink opened in Duchton when they were seven years old. They had a few lessons when they first started and learned the basics. After that, they took off on their own. Some of the most fun Jana can remember here is when one of her boys twirls her toward another one who will help her land a small jump sending her to another one of her boys. She trusts them and can close her eyes and let the dance play out in her mind pretending she is a prima ballerina.

They love activities which keep them physically fit. Sweating, even if it's in the cold, they slow for a minute. Jana says, "Let's get a cup of hot chocolate and rest."

They leave the rink and head over to one of the many vendors and buy hot drinks and roasted nuts. While they're sitting there, Jana feels a presence, and a chill runs down her spine. She glances around for the reason when she hears

Greyd say, "Stacy, we can't talk here. Will you follow us to the bathroom?"

Greyd walks toward the bathroom, and the others are hot on his heels. They make it to the boys' bathroom. JoeJoe checks then comes back shaking his head to them that it's not clear.

Stacy tells Asa, "The girl's room is empty." Asa leads the way into the lady's restroom. Jana checks it, and it is clear. Once inside, they lock the door behind them.

Asa says, "Stacy's getting restless and wants to move on. She's wondering if we've told the police who the murderer is yet or not."

Jana tells her what had happened with Detective Walsh and says, "Stacy, it will be a few more days. We have to do this, so they believe us and don't arrest us, instead. Do you mind giving us the time we need?"

Asa answers them as a translator would, "Stacy says she doesn't mind waiting a little longer. She thinks another spirit is following her and is very sneaky. She wants to know if she can help us by trying to figure out what that spirit wants."

Asa answers her, "Thank you, Stacy, we'd appreciate the feedback and any information you can get would be great."

Just then someone bumps hard into the door, cursing, "Mother fucker, that hurt! What in the hell is this door locked for? Shit!"

Chagrined, Kaden reaches out, turns the lock to the open position and pulls open the door just wide enough for one person to go through. Jana walks out keeping her head tucked to avoid the withering glare of the intruder who watches Jana leave, while rubbing her shoulder. The outraged interloper decides to tell Jana what for and starts a lecture, "Young lady, let me tell you—"

Asa walks out then, and the busybody abruptly ends her prepared insult, beginning a whole new one for Jana and Asa,

"Well, I never …" Her angry eyes are little more than slits, her large brows pinched together in a way that looks almost painful. But now her face has taken on a deep shade of crimson. Her glare remains intense as the two. …

Greydan walks out. The meddler has ended her crusade of attack of another faster than it began. Her eyes are now wide, and her mouth has fallen open, quivering as if she's still trying to speak, but the words don't make it from her brain into her mouth.

When JoeJoe walks out, nosey's forehead, once tight with scorn pouring upon Jana and Asa is now relaxed. Her eyes wide with shock, twitch from Jana to each of the boys again and again. The stranger's mouth remains wholly open and unmoving. She's also stopped rubbing her shoulder and is simply holding her hand on it; any idea of pain now lost in stunned disbelief of what she's witnessing.

When Kaden walks out, the previously furious woman, once so prepared to toss verbal insults at the beautiful young Jana, falls backward onto a couch in the hallway before the door. The trauma of her worldview crashing around her obviously too much for her to handle.

Jana smiles. She and her boys keep their heads down and head to the parking lot.

They had skated through lunch with a break for hot chocolate and roasted nuts. Needless to say, they're hungry, especially JoeJoe and Asa. As skinny as Asa is, he can eat more than any of the others, even JoeJoe, who at six feet four inches is the biggest of the teens. Still, the soft brown-haired Elf Boy can out eat him on most occasions.

The crew decides to go back to Maize's Restaurant and grab some old-fashioned burgers and fries. On the way, they drive past the truck stop and rest area. Each of them senses the vibration of the universe change around them as they near the scene of the murder. Each of them chooses to say nothing, knowing how the others feel because of their deep understanding of one another.

When they get to the diner, JoeJoe holds the door for the others, and Kaden leads the group to a booth in the back. Jana sits between Asa and JoeJoe. *This should be fun. I'll need to order extra because it's a sure bet one of these two will help me. One or both of them will eat what I don't finish.*

True to form JoeJoe orders the biggest burger they offer, a double patty, double bacon, with mustard, tomatoes, pickles, lettuce, onion, and an extra-large order of extra crispy French fries. Asa orders the same, only mayo and no onion. He's thinking of kisses later. There isn't a person in the group who doesn't wonder how Asa stays so thin with as much as he eats. Greyd gets a cheeseburger, loaded, and fries. Kaden orders a club sandwich with extra bacon. Finally, Jana orders the nachos. She always orders the large nachos, which she shares with all of her boys. When she finishes all that she wants she scoots her plate closer to Asa. He grins and starts eating the leftover nachos. JoeJoe puts his hand on her leg close to her knee. She's warmed by his big hand. When she puts hers on top of his, she's rewarded with a slight lift at the corner of his lips.

Jana asks, "I have to do chores. I told my mom that I would clean out my closet this weekend. You all are welcome to come if you want, but I need to go."

Asa pipes up, "Sounds good. I'll follow you home. Then, I have to check on my house and bring in the mail. I'll be back to see you before bedtime." The others also go their separate ways, each needing to get work finished at their own homes.

❦

THAT NIGHT, Asa and Jana are snuggling together. Jana asks, "Asa, do you think your parents might let you stay here with me after my parents move? I'm not looking forward to being here alone."

"I don't think it'll be a problem, honey. In fact, mom and dad haven't been home in so long that if I move in with you, they'll probably sell our house and travel even more. I won't leave you alone, and I'm sure the others won't, either."

"Thank you!" she says, then snuggles into him and falls asleep.

Asa wakes her in the morning with the smell of coffee. He hands her a cup, black with two sugars, as she walks through the kitchen on her way to the bathroom to shower and get ready for school. Sipping her coffee as she moves, she makes her way mostly by muscle memory, her eyes just slits. She steps into the shower and is almost finished when she senses someone in the room with her.

Jana calls out, "Asa, what are you doing? Is everything okay?" She pokes her head out of the shower and sees that no one is there, then talks to herself, "That's just crazy. I thought someone was in here for a second."

She tucks a fluffy towel around her and thinks maybe one of her parents stayed home from work today. They're usually gone by six-thirty to make it on time. She thinks she had better check on them once she's dressed. She cautiously looks at her image in the mirror and finds only herself. Calming, she puts on a little makeup and starts on her hair. After she finishes drying and brushing her hair, she walks down the hall to her parents' room. Their bed is made up, and no one is in the place.

That odd feeling is making her stomach roll some, and like she has been doing for days, she avoids looking in her mom's big dresser mirror as she passes it.

Asa calls to her, making her jump. As she gets close to him, he says, "Happy Birthday, beautiful girl." He gives her a tight hug then says, "Hun, do you want to ride to school with me and save a little gas, or do you need to drive?"

"I'd rather ride with you, but, if Kaden's dad calls, I might need a ride to meet him after school. Could you take me?"

"Sure, I can. I have an appointment to pick up a schedule for a shoot before the fall formal. It's for some advertising for formal teen clothes or something like that for all the winter wear coming out. It'll just take me a couple of minutes. You can go in with me if you'd like."

"I'd love to see where you work, Elf Boy. Do they have any nude pics of you on the walls?"

He shakes his head, smiling a little-lopsided grin, and he motions her to the front door with a wave of his hand.

13

MAKING A MARK

The school day started normally and went downhill from there. The teachers who had been easy on homework Friday, piled it on extra to make up for the easy day. The whole group will have homework, there's just too much to get it all finished at school. Stress is high, and several of the school's bullies are in fine form, causing as many problems in the hallways as they possibly can.

JoeJoe has it especially hard from bullies because all the smaller boys with 'little man' syndrome want to vent by 'taking down the big guy' and in doing so, make themselves a good reputation for being tough. JoeJoe's been sitting in the principal's office most of the morning because he picked up three smaller guys, who were picking on him, all at once. He set them in an area reserved for teacher's decor which is actually a shelf in the wall. He was about to miss his lunch when Mrs. Scott, the principal, told him to get out of her office and from now on just gently guide the smaller bullies to her office.

The crew is waiting for him at their usual table, wondering where he is, when he walks up and says, "I'm sure getting tired of being messed with by the little guys. If any of you have any pull with them, can you get them off of my back?" to which the entire group busts out laughing.

Jana says, "I'll protect you, big guy. Just text me when you start to get into trouble." He chuffs, bumps her with his shoulder, and they start eating.

Kaden tells them, "I'll do what I can. I hope you're ready for the news my dad just texted. He wants to know if we can be at the station after school. What should I tell him?"

Jana answers, "I can, but it'll take me … let's see, I have to go with Asa to get his schedule on the way, and that's about ten minutes out of the way, so it will take us twenty there and back. Tell him we should be there around four o'clock. Is that good with the rest of you guys?"

They all agree to the time Jana set, then go about finishing the rest of the school day without any other issues. After the final bell rings, they meet in the parking lot and load their books into their cars before heading off.

Greydan says, "I'll stop for drinks. Does anyone want anything?" Everyone tells him what they want. It's something they think of before using their gifts because sometimes they get involved and use up their energy. It's especially tricky on Jana. She can get weak and shaky if she isn't careful. The guys are bigger and can power through.

When Jana and Asa arrive at the modeling agency, he gets out and takes his girl's hand to help her out of the truck. They walk into his place of work, hand in hand. He stops to speak to a gorgeous dark-skinned woman, "Jana, this is my friend, Marjani. She's from Ethiopia. Marjani, this is my girlfriend, Jana."

Jana answers first, "It's nice to meet you, Marjani."

With an English accent, Marjani responds, "Thank you, Miss Jana. It's wonderful to meet you as well." Jana smiles and lets Asa pull her away.

"See you later," Asa says, walking away from the front desk and his friend.

"I'm looking forward to it, Asa," she replies.

"She is stunning! I almost couldn't speak," Jana says.

"Well, get used to it around here. You can't swing a cat without hitting someone prettier than the last person. The good thing is most of them don't let it go to their head."

Jana laughs.

"What's so funny, honey?"

Jana rolls her eyes at his unintended unfunny pun. "What, like you don't fit in with all of these beautiful people?"

"Well, I don't really give it much—"

Just then Jana hears a whistle. An older gentleman saunters up and shakes Asa's hand while looking at Jana. He says, "So, is this your girl, young man? I have to say you couldn't have done better. Young lady, are you looking for a modeling job? I think you two could make for some amazing couples' advertising."

Asa's eyes get big, and he sends a questioning look Jana's way but says nothing.

Jana answers for herself, "I have a busy schedule, but I might accept on a one-time basis if I can work it into my schedule Mr.––"

The tall man answers, "Davis, Kevin Davis, here's my card, and I'll remember you." He's busy but hands a printed schedule and tickets to Asa, explaining that he needs him on Saturday for a shoot by the ocean. Asa nods, he is known for being on time and ready, so no words are necessary. He motions for Jana to leave. He takes her hand, and they walk back to his truck.

The next stop is the police station. Going inside, they stop and sit in the visitor area, waiting on the others. Kaden's the next to arrive, holding the door open for Greydan and JoeJoe. After saying hello, he waves for them all to follow him to his dad's office. The desk officer notices him and the others, and he knows they're expected. He's familiar with Kaden, so he doesn't question him as he passes into the precinct.

The tall dark-headed Kaden taps on his dad's closed door, opens it, then stands aside while motioning the others in. It isn't the most prominent office, but it's big enough that they aren't squeezed in. There are only two chairs, so they can't all sit. Besides, they've been sitting all day. Mr. Walsh is smiling when he greets them but turns all business when the door closes.

He says, "JoeJoe, as a confidential informant, I want you to know we're very secure here, and your information and name will be protected. We have no paperwork and will only add that we received information of a report from a good source that the police will investigate. Their facts will be entered into evidence. I've already put the information that I heard from you into a report and given it the DA on the Perrin case. They will … if they haven't already, talk to my superiors about it. Do you have anything else you need to add? I've said in my report my informant is a reliable adult and that's enough."

"I understand, Mr. Walsh, and I have no problem. I have nothing to hide that you probably don't already know, and nothing to add," Kaden says.

"Now, Jana, this is a little bit different for you. I did talk to the DA about using a psychic, he has a special fund that his office hasn't touched in years for just such cases and is ready to use it. He wants to hire your services and will meet with you now if you give the word. While we're waiting for him, I need you to talk to an artist here on the force that works with a computer program to make a sketch of the perp. If you don't mind?"

"No sir, I don't mind at all," Jana responds, do you mind if

Greydan or the other boys go with me? We operate as a team, we are dependent on each other when in the field."

"Will you tell me a little more about what 'in the field' means, please?" the detective asks.

"Yes, sir. For as long as we've known each other, we've been doing things to help others with our gifts. Sometimes, they are spirits who haven't been able to move on or families who call us, afraid of a spirit that might be in their home and needs to be removed. It could be as simple as a plant in the yard, a little salt, a prayer, or many times just asking the spirit to leave. Other times have been especially hard. One such time was just last week." Jana goes on to tell Kaden's father what happened at the Gordon's that wasn't said to the police that night.

Henry Walsh becomes very serious as he says, "How did I miss this for your whole lives? I feel like I've missed too much. I thought I knew you all very well. Now this information, I want to know that you're all safe. Will you make me a deal? The next time you think something might be even just a little dangerous, you will call first and let me know?"

All the crew answers that they will. Mr. Walsh looks at them for a few moments, then decides if they want, they could lie to him, and he wouldn't know it, so he nods his thanks and gets up. "Jana, please come this way. Boys, I'm afraid only one of you can go with her. So, Greydan, if that's you, please follow me." The two teens nod at the others.

Kaden says, "We'll meet you at Maize's when you're finished."

Jana and Greydan meet an officer named McDaniels. She walks them through the process of making the sketch. They know precisely what the person they want to describe looks like, so they're not hesitant, and the job is completed quickly. Officer McDaniels prints the picture and verifies, "You're sure this picture is an accurate representation of what the man in your physic vision looks like?

The teens don't need Asa to know that Officer McDaniels seriously doubts the validity of Jana's gift. The two of them pass it off like water off a duck's back. It doesn't matter to them as long as they're happy they did their best to help. In this case, they are trying to get a murderer off of the streets, and in doing so, help Stacy move on. It might also help Stacy's family by putting to rest some of their questions and fears. So yeah, they are okay with someone who doesn't believe in them. When the officer finishes, they go back the way they came and give a copy of the sketch to detective Walsh.

Jana says, "Mr. Walsh, if you need us, you have our numbers. You can also tell Kaden if you want, and he'll call us."

"I don't know how to thank you for this. Let me show you the way out."

Having completed at least part of the more public aspect of their outreach to the police in their search for justice for Stacy's murder, Greydan and Jana follow compliantly behind Henry Walsh. Neither teen has any illusion their statements will be held as the gospel truth from the majority of the leadership in the precinct. They do, however, believe that they have taken an essential first step in bringing their skills into the light. Jana secretly hopes it will make it easier on them moving forward. The young clairvoyant doesn't surmise what they do will be mainstream in the near future. She has hopes that today will serve as an awakening, and they won't have to hide their gifts forever.

Just before they reach the door separating the public areas of the station from the private sectors, Greyd surreptitiously tugs on the back of Jana's coat. They're very much in tune with one another.

Instinctively, Jana knows that her blue-eyed football jock has seen a spirit nearby. She watches him for a direction to look. After verifying where, her response to him is equally as subtle with slight nod and smile in the direction he had pointed. Using a minor uptick of his chin he tells the spirit they see him. With that, Greyd holds open the door for Jana, smiles, and waves at the spirit then says, "We'll be back soon."

The spirit nods in understanding, then like a policeman directing traffic, waves to them as they leave the room. Anyone who saw the interaction either live or on a recording would believe Greyd is waving to Mr. Walsh.

"If I need something, I'll reach out. Bye, kids," the detective says.

14

IN THIS CAR

*G*reyd drives Jana to Maize's Restaurant. He hops out and opens the door for her. Before she can start for the diner, Greyd pulls her in close to him and says, "We've had some great memories in this car, haven't we, baby? I think we need a picture. Let's take a selfie in front of her, okay? I'm sure my parents are getting me a car for my birthday next month, so this one will go soon."

"How wonderful, Greyd! Yes, handsome, I'll take a picture with you. Our first kiss was in this car. I'll never forget her, either." His baby blues melt her to the core as she stares up into his face, smiling.

Greyd holds his phone out with his long-muscled arm. He taps several times, taking several pictures. Then he quickly sends them to Jana's phone in a text that says; my beautiful girl smiling at me. Jana tiptoes up with her hand on his chest and pulls his face down to hers. Touching him gives her tingles in her belly, but kissing him has her breath hitching. She decides they'd better get inside to the others quickly. Greyd grudgingly turns her loose, and they hold hands and walk to the entrance of the restaurant.

The others saved them seats and are eagerly awaiting their arrival. A tall, pretty waitress comes over and asks for their drink order. Water with a lemon wedge for Jana and cola for Greydan. JoeJoe has cola in front of him, Kaden an unsweetened tea and there's an empty chocolate milkshake in front of Asa. The waitress is new and, unlike the other workers, doesn't know what they always order. She's a young waitress who takes their food order smiling and walks away without writing it down.

Jana snickers, "She'll get a vote from me if she can remember our order without checking with us two or three times." The guys agree.

When she returns with Jana and Greyd's drinks, she also brings a refill for Asa. She sits it in front of him and says, "This is from me."

Surprised, Asa looks at her and simply says, "Thank you."

The young lady blushes and winks at him. This all plays out in front of Jana, who isn't worried. Other girls don't hold any interest in Asa. He's found his perfect partner and has no intention of going out with anyone else.

Greydan gets up and goes to the restroom. Asa slips sideways into his chair neatly placing his arm around Jana as he does. When the waitress returns her playful mask is replaced with a professional but disappointed look. The letdown is as apparent as her flirting. She asks, "May I get any of you anything else?"

Jana, looking directly at her tells her says, "No, but thank you." She hopes it comes across as earnestly as it's meant and relieves a little of the rejection's sting.

JoeJoe asks, "How was the drive over?"

Jana, recognizes the question is a ploy to bring the group's attention to each other and let the waitress leave with her head high. She launches a long-ago story of this lousy driver who cut them off. They all have these stories,

They use them to deflect interest. The stuff is true and did happen … at least at some point, they happened to one of them just not today.

After the waitress is gone and Greydan returns, Jana shares the process of the police artist making the sketch.

Greydan tells them about the ghost in the police station they need to help as soon as they can. He doesn't use the word ghost but their code of using a car instead. "So, we are there, and take the white car out for a spin. Maybe you guys can tell me if the engine needs any help or not. What do you think?"

Jana says, "I'm in sounds great." Murmurs of agreement and bobs of four heads follow her statement. Using the car code causes her to ask, "Hey, Greyd, what kind of car are you getting next month, anyway?"

"My parents said it's my pick. What do you guys think? I want something sporty, but something that'll still carry as many of us as possible."

JoeJoe pipes up, "Really, get what you want, I did. If four of us can fit in Asa's matchbox truck, we can fit in anything if we have to, buddy." JoeJoe's eighteenth birthday was September the 24th, and his parents got him a big four-wheel drive Dodge Ram truck, trying to accommodate his tall body. Greydan told him it was to fit his massive head. In any case, the truck is big enough the others fit comfortably, and they love its smooth ride. JoeJoe promised he would take them to do donuts in the school parking lot during Christmas break when it snows enough.

After JoeJoe explains what 'doing a donut' is, Jana can't wait. She likes going fast. In fact, park rides which make others sick are her favorite, the boys love to take her to parks that have them. Asa goes to have a caramel apple or five and JoeJoe for the funnel cakes, but mostly they go because their girl gets so excited.

One time at a theme park, Jana was shooting the water guns at a target, and a playful spirit came and told Asa, "If your girlfriend really wants to win, she should shoot the one on the end. It's the only one set up to really work right with the gun." Asa, being the good boyfriend that he is, immediately told Jana what the phantom had told him. Unfortunately for the game operator, Jana can't stand liars or cheats. So, she sat down on the last stool and won the game ten times in a row. She was readying herself to leave when the barker tried to bully her out. Wrong move. She won another thirteen times to show the jerk he shouldn't cheat people. Then whispered to the next player how to win and asked them to pass it along when they left.

"I'll be right back, guys," Jana says to excuse herself to go to the bathroom. She's washing up when she sees a young lady trying to get her attention from inside the mirror. Her panicked eyes, wide and intense, stare unblinking at Jana as she drums furiously on the other side of the glass. Jana asks her what she can do for her. The woman half turns away and appears to have heard something. She abruptly disappears from the view fading into a silvery mist in seconds.

Jana is shaking but speaks to the reflecting surface, "I'm sorry I didn't get to speak with you. Should I wait, or will you find me again? Give me a sign if you'll find me again."

Nothing … no response. Not a cold breeze, noise, or even smell to give Jana cause to believe the girl in the mirror heard her. Jana waits. She knows Asa already knows what's happened and what is going on. Wait … there is something. A smell of flowers. More precisely, poets' daffodils! They're Jana's favorite flower. She helped her mom plant a whole backyard garden full of them when she was little. Jana looks around and finds … nothing.

The only other bathroom smells are cleaning agents. Satisfied, she faces the mirror and says, "Thank you. I'll go for now, but I'll be looking for you. We're trying to figure out a way to get to you safely, so we can free you." Jana smells the scent of the daffodils even more than before. As she pulls open the bathroom door open to leave, the waitress who had flirted with Asa pushes in. It's an awkward moment as they bump into each other. There's the inevitable dance and apologies as they fix their positions.

The pretty waitress stops and says, "I really want to apologize for flirting with your boyfriend. I didn't realize you were a couple." She gazes with a look of awe at Jana.

"It's no problem. He is gorgeous, isn't he?" Jana says with obvious pride.

"Yes, he is… may I ask you something … something personal?" She asked nervously, while quickly adding, "You don't have to answer if you don't want to."

"Yes, of course. I don't mind."

"Are they all with you? I mean they all look like they like you, but are all of them your boyfriends?"

Jana gives the girl the benefit of the doubt that she really just wants to know and isn't judging. Curiosity in and of itself isn't a problem, but the gossip and judgment of some people is. "Well, first you should know my name, and maybe you could tell me yours. My name is Jana." She sticks her hand out while looking the girl directly in the eyes.

"Oh, no! My manners are horrible! You're right. What was I thinking? My name is Erin. It's nice to meet you. I'm sorry about the manners. I really am not that kind of a person. I'm just curious."

The young clairvoyant is laughing at the situation she and Erin have found themselves. So, she decides to go all in, "Yes, I'm dating them all. They're all my boyfriends. Your manners are fine. Trust me, I get turned around like that too."

"Thanks, Jana. I promise I will not flirt with any of them now that I know they're taken. I've only lived in Duchton for about five months. Getting resettled from the move has taken up almost all of my free time. I've only just now been able to get this job. Seriously, they're all gorgeous. Give a girl some pointers?"

"I'd be happy to help, but you have work, and I have to get back to my guys. We have a birthday party planned later this month, though. Would you like to come and maybe meet some of our friends?"

"Oh, yes, I'd love to! Thank you," Erin says, a tear streaking down her face at odds with her genuine laughter.

Jana quickly grabs a paper towel from the dispenser.

"Here, take this. I'm sure you're happy … right?"

"Yes! It's just I've been here all this time and have no friends. Then the girl whose boyfriend I was just hitting on is being nice to me … sorry, it hit all at once. I didn't see it coming." More laughter follows then she adds, "Jana, I'm excited, and will do my best to be there!"

Jana puts a hand in the air, and Erin slaps it with one of her own. "I'll bring you an invite in the next few days. If I forget and you see me, remind me, okay? I have a lot going on right now."

"I will, and thanks again," Erin said.

Watching her boys as she makes it back to the table, Jana tries not drool. Yes, they are scorching guys!

Standing by the table, Jana says, "Hey, guys, I really need to talk outside … do you mind?" She knows that Greyd or JoeJoe, wait, was this one Kaden's turn? … maybe Asa's … whoever; someone has already paid. Asa has surely already let them know that something happened, and they would need to be ready to go when she returned. They guys nod at her and get up to leave.

Carol, from the bar, shouts, "Thank y'all, and come back!"

They all yell back a chorus of, "Thank you, Carol. Bye. See you later."

They walk to the back of Greydan's car. Asa nods that no one is listening, so after telling them about the girl in the mirror, Jana says, "I have a feeling she's one of the prisoners. We need to talk about what we've each discovered to get on with their rescue."

Kaden says, "We can get on it tomorrow if dad doesn't have us helping the DA. I guess even that doesn't matter. We should meet at Jana's to talk."

"Hey, I'll make dinner. That is if you want me to," Jana teases them.

The vote is unanimous. They vote for her famous lasagna and garlic bread. Then the teens all split off and go home for the night.

15

CALLING HIS PARENTS

*S*chool is just another typical day—lather, rinse, repeat. That's until the crew gathers for lunch. JoeJoe already found a table for them and is waiting with a big tray of food in front of him.

Erie High has its share of bullies. These guys like to play 'take on the bigger guys,' knowing if the larger guy responds, he'll be the one in trouble for not walking away or telling a teacher.

JoeJoe is waiting at their table when Donny, one of the more notorious school bullies, tries to take his food. "No, Donny, you're not taking this," JoeJoe says calmly, holding the tray with his big hands. "This is for my friends and me. If you want something, I'll get it, but from now on you can ask if you want something."

Donny replies, "Fuck you, Doporto. I want it, and you're going to give it to me, now!"

Jana and Greydan enter the cafeteria just in time to see the start of the altercation. Greydan hurries over, loudly asking, "Is there a problem here, JoeJoe?" then he aggressively pushes into Donny's space, towering over the punk. The bully doesn't say a word, he just squares up and socks Greydan in the face striking him in the nose. There's an awful crunch, and blood spurts everywhere before he falls to the floor.

Greydan jumps straight up and starts for the little bully but is pulled back by Asa who had walked in behind him. The surrounding students are up in a flash chanting, "Fight, fight, fight."

Skinny Asa can hold his friend but only just. Then the teacher on lunch duty hurries to the fight. He puts his hand on the smaller bully's chest, pushing him away from the struggling Greydan. He glances around and tells both of the boys to head to the office pointing to Donny and warning, "I'll be behind you the whole way, Donny. Don't even think about getting out of line."

Donny leads the way with a predictable shit-eating grin on his face as he low-fives his friends while he struts his way through the students on the way to the principal's office.

Jana walks with Greyd. JoeJoe is right behind them. She'd snagged some napkins and gives them to her guy to press around his nose. It doesn't seem to be stopping, and the bleeding appears quite severe. Jana shoves a water cup under his nose and the gushing blood pools in the bottom of the container. "It looks bad, JoeJoe, I'm worried," Jana says.

Asa and Kaden left the tray full of food and are following after Greydan to the office.

"Hey, all you kids, back to your classes now," says the teacher, taking Greydan and Donny to the principal's office. None of them listen and follow along anyway. The teacher decides it isn't worth the fight, turns and keeps walking.

Asa says, "JoeJoe, help Greyd, he's feeling woozy."

JoeJoe gets to him at the same time his brother wilts. Greydan would've hit the floor without JoeJoe to catch him, but his quick reaction was primed by the prescient warning from Asa.

JoeJoe carries him straight through the school doors and out to his truck with the teacher screaming at their backs. Like his rant about them leaving Greydan with him, Jana, JoeJoe, Kaden, and Asa pay him no mind. They've got another destination in mind.

As they arrive at the main hospital ER, Greyd is out cold, so JoeJoe carries him into the emergency room.

The nurse says, "What is—?"

But the big boy never stops. He goes up to the doors and shouts, "Let us in now!" She buzzes the door open and immediately walks around the counter and tells the young people that only two of them can go with him. Kaden and Asa don't so much as bat an eye as JoeJoe and Jana take their friend back. They retreat to the familiar waiting room. They have, after all, been here many times over the years of the quintet's friendship.

Kaden calls his dad, first. Kaden knows his dad will know what they should do. He says, "Dad, a kid at school bloodied Greydan's nose, and he's bleeding way too much for a typical nose bleed. We brought him to the ER. I'm calling the Sayers next. And dad, that kid who hit Greydan is a known bully, the school might be calling the police if they haven't already."

Detective Walsh's answer is full of compassion as he answers, "Don't worry, son, I'll call the Sayers and the school, so they know why you kids left. Stay there and wait for the Sayers. I'll call you back in a little while."

When the young Walsh puts up his phone, Asa watches him and says, "Your dad says he's calling the Sayers and then he'll call the school. They'll be lucky if the Sayers don't sue the city over this or press charges of their own."

"Probably both," Kaden adds.

Asa says as an afterthought, "I bet this means no lasagna tonight."

❦

THE NURSES SHOW JoeJoe where to place his still bleeding brother. He's on a bed in an upright position to keep the blood from running down his throat. They're in a pretty large room considering it's in an emergency room. One nurse asks JoeJoe and Jana to stand out of the way at the front of the room where they are now. They stand quiet as a white-haired doctor rushes in and takes a look at their friend. He's looking at the machines that are being attached to Greyd when he notices the clear water cup filled with blood in Jana's hands. Dawning realization on his face, he asks, "Is that is from your friend's nose?"

Jana nods her head up and down.

Then the doctor asks, "How did this happen?"

Jana answers, "A school bully punched him in the nose."

The doctor nods and grunts, "Uh, ha," and tells the nurse, "This is a severe Epistaxis he needs a stat X-ray." Turning back to Jana and JoeJoe, his questions continue, "Do you know if he's had aspirin or if he's a free bleeder?"

JoeJoe quickly responds, "Yes he did have some aspirin after practice this morning. Greydan took a big hit to his knee and coach let him take some. He's not a free bleeder."

The two friends had to move out of the way as the X-ray technician hurries in with the portable x-ray machine.

Jana has tears running in waves down her face. One of the nurses puts a hand on her shoulder, "You did the right thing. This is serious. But he's very well taken care of. We need you to go to the waiting room now. I promise I'll let you know in just a few minutes what is happening with your friend." This same nurse guides them to the door, and they both walk out to meet with the others.

Asa's face turns green.

Kaden notices and panics a bit, asking, "Is he alright? Guys, is he alright?" his voice raising.

JoeJoe says, "Yes but they said it's serious. Even the doctor looked worried. They told us we did the right thing bringing him in, and he's in good hands. They'll come out and tell us soon how he is."

In just minutes, Ricky Sayer rushes into the waiting room. Swiveling around he finds his son JoeJoe and his friends, he heads straight over to them. Without any pleasantries and in rapid-fire, he asks, "How's Greydan? Where is he?" He examines the members of the little quartet when he sees a nurse appear at the nurse's station. Without awaiting an answer to his questions and with zero hesitation, he turns and hastens directly toward the unsuspecting caregivers.

JoeJoe, knowing his father's worry and frustration at needing to see his son stalks over, puts a hand on him, and says, "They're doing an X-ray. Dad, he's in good care. They know what they are doing. Come sit with us, and I'll tell you everything."

As Mr. Sayer sits, his wife, Lucy, runs in through the sliding glass hospital doors. So quick is her entrance that she has to sidestep the final entry, to not run right into it. Rick Sayer rises and walks with deliberation over to his wife. His demeanor has changed dramatically as if sensing his wife's panic, he's now taken on the face of the protective, calm husband. He wraps her in his arms, telling her almost word for word what JoeJoe had just told him. They both sit, listening as the group of teenagers relates the story from the beginning. When the teens finish, the anger and disgust fixed on the Sayers' faces make it evident that the school and the bully are about to have a tough time.

"The first question I have is what is the bully's name?" asks the fuming Rick.

"Donny White," answers Jana, maybe a little too happily.

Lucy asks, "Where were the teachers while this altercation was starting?" The kids shake their heads, showing they don't know.

Then Jana says, "We don't know, but when Donny hit Greyd, Mr. Henkel showed up and got between them, making Donny stop. Asa was holding onto Greydan, so it was just the one hit. Greyd never hit the boy. He didn't touch him at all, in fact."

The white-haired doctor enters the waiting room with a bit of a flourish, opening both doors to come into the room. "Greydan Sayer."

The Sayers stand, so the doctor comes over to the group and says, "Are you the parents?"

"Yes," the Sayers state in unison.

"He's doing just fine and will be able to see you soon. Greydan took a bad hit to his nose which broke it. As it did, it nicked an artery. Several things compounded the problem causing it to become serious. The weather changing, he had aspirin today, and he is a little anemic. Greydan's lost too much blood and needs a transfusion. His blood type is O positive, do you want me to order blood from the blood bank or do you want to give the blood?"

With the type of instant decision that Rick Sayer is famous for, he says, "I'll give the blood for my son. Just tell me what to do."

The doctor says, "Come this way, and, Mrs. Sayer, you can come and sit with him if you would like while we are getting the blood."

She nods then answers, "Yes." Turning to the teens, she says, "I'll be back soon to let you know how he is and let you go back to see him, too."

They leave the teens to talk among themselves. It's only a little while before the Sayers are back and let JoeJoe and Jana go in.

Lucy says, "He's awake and feels fine, he says, but he looks awful, though." I want to thank you all for your quick thinking. JoeJoe, you saved your brother's life. It could've been much worse if the bleeding weren't stopped as quickly as it was."

Now that the whole day is gone, the kids get ready to go their separate ways. Letting Greyd go was very hard for Jana. She wants to stay with him but understands that what he needs most is rest. The doctor admitted him to the hospital out of an abundance of caution for overnight observation. "Not that anything is wrong, but with a transfusion, we want to be careful," he had said.

Anyway, Jana and the boys will be able to see Greyd tomorrow after school, at home. "He has his phone, so if he texts, we can text him back," Jana says.

"Him first, though, so we're not waking him. It's been a long day," adds Kaden.

"You guys ... it just hit me. Now that this disaster is over, I just remembered today was when Stacy Perrin's parents had set her funeral," says Asa.

"We'll make it up to them," replies Jana, "we'll make it up to them by finding her killer. Maybe we can send them a card and let them know why we missed it, too," she adds with little enthusiasm. Their parents did send flowers, that's good enough for now.

16

CONSEQUENCES

*J*ana's been walking in a haze all morning. Thank goodness, Asa drove her to school. She might not have gotten there safely if she had tried to drive on her own. Dragging into her class with Mr. Janes, she sits down beside her Elf Boy who puts a hand on her leg. Jana's thinking of sneaking a quick text to Greyd, but this is one class where she will get in trouble if caught with her phone.

Mr. Janes is different from most of their teachers. Instead of taking their phones and putting them in the front of the room or threatening oral reports or worse, this teacher rewards them for good behavior. He tells them if they do their work and their phone stays silent, they can choose prizes at the end of each chapter from a prize shelf. This shelf's where he has lots of great things on display that most teens want. Even something as simple as a new pair of earbuds is something to keep their phones off in this class.

Jana has her eye on some of the classic books that are in the collection of goodies. She notices a new book on the supernatural aspects of mirrors, and her eyes widen. She walks up to Mr. Janes desk with the book in her hands and asks, "Mr. Janes, can I read this if I bring it back before the end of the month? I'll keep my phone off and in my pocket. Anyway, this is what I'll want if you let me have a reward at the end of the month."

The older teacher smiles at his student and says, "Miss Jay, you can have it now just pay me back by doing what you said and keeping your grades up, and your phone put away. I'll trust you."

The young lady walks off with a smile. It's much harder for her to keep the book closed than it is to stay off of her phone. Asa tells her on the way out, "It's amazing that he would have that book, not that series of gargoyle books you wanted."

Jana laughs and tightens her grip on his arm.

"You're fantastic, too, for noticing it and asking for it! That book might just have some of the answers we're looking for.

The bell rings, and they walk out with the other students Asa's hand on his girl's back. Most of the students at Erie High know that Jana has four boyfriends and are okay with it. It wasn't that way in the past, but now it's not a worry. Most of the other students stay away from them because they're different. Their relationship status plays only a small role in their lack of meaningful relationships outside of their little cadre.

She feels a slight buzz on her cute little butt from her phone and jerks it out reads a message from Greyd.

I'm home and doing fine. Have JoeJoe get everyone here after school. Okay? I'd like to see everyone.

He has put several emojis after the message including kissy hearts.

Jana takes a deep breath and sighs. She shows Asa the message in the group chat with a smile, making sure he sees it then responds to Greyd. The feeling of relief washes over her as she taps out the text.

I'll make sure everyone gets there myself. We'll be there as soon as school's out. I can't wait to hold you.

Asa taps a message, too, it's just emojis and even more kissy hearts!

FEELING MUCH BETTER, Jana and Asa walk to her reading class where he steals a kiss before telling her he'll see her at lunch as he leaves to go to his own class. The boys always make sure one of them is in a class with her, and math is no different. JoeJoe's already seated, waiting for her when she walks in, her white teeth flashing a broad smile at him. He looks up, obviously glad to see her. Before she sits beside him, she stands in front of him and rubs his muscular shoulders, still grinning from ear to ear, relief evident in every angle of her face. JoeJoe looks tired and has big bags under his dark eyes.

Recognizing his exhaustion, Jana asks, "You didn't sleep, did you, big guy? Are you okay? I'll go and get you some juice if you think it'll help."

He answers, "No don't worry about me, beautiful, I'll be alright now that Greyd's home. Mom's off work. She took the week off and told them if he isn't better she'll take the next week, too." He chuckles.

Jana loves JoeJoes's laugh. He isn't one who wears his feelings for the world to see. Hearing his laughter is a relief, and her worry for him takes a step down the priority ladder.

The overhead speakers pop, and the students hear, "This is vice principal Owens, and I request the presence of JoeJoe Doporto in my office ASAP."

Jana looks up into JoeJoe's eyes, "Don't let him push you around. You didn't do anything wrong."

JoeJoe stares back at his pretty girlfriend. "Beautiful, I got this. Don't worry, he won't push me around. Besides, Greyd is going to be fine. Owens can't mess up my day!" His smile is warm as he stands to take a hall pass from the teacher's assistant at the door. All eyes in the class are on him as he nods to Jana and leaves.

When he gets to the office, he signs in and sits to wait. It's only a few minutes before the vice-principal, Mr. Owens calls him into his office. JoeJoe notices the school security officer waiting outside the door. He sits as instructed and waits.

"Mr. Doporto, you caused quite a stir yesterday. First, starting a fight, then walking away from Mr. Henkel, and finally, taking your brother off of school property. Before I decide on punishment, I'd like to know what you have to say for yourself?"

JoeJoe says nothing but holds up his left index finger in the universal 'hold on' gesture. As he does, he reaches into his back pocket for his phone with his right hand. Retrieving it, he speed dials his dad, who answers on the first ring. "Dad, vice-principal Owens has me seated in his office with a security guard at the door. He's about to punish me for taking Greyd to the hospital yesterday ..." there is a short pause before he says, "Yes, sir."

The big teen lowers his finger, and while staring a hole through his prosecutor's eyes, he says, "My dad will be here in fifteen minutes. He told me not to tell you anything and that he'll bring my lawyer with him."

Anger boils off of the self-important vice principal, and he responds with, "That is not always wise, boy, to go whining to your father. You go wait in the front office for him."

"Well, it's always wise to put a bully in his place." JoeJoe stands and goes to the front office as he was told.

When Ricky Sayer strolls into the office, he says, "JoeJoe, walk with us please, son. I want you to be here for this." He walks straight past the school secretary and into the vice-principal's office without knocking.

Mr. Owens hangs up his phone and watches the men with disdain until Mr. Sayer starts, "I understand that you want to punish my son, Harry?"

"I haven't decided yet, Mr. Sayer. We were only beginning our discussion when he rudely interrupted me and called you."

"Ah, I understand how you would like this to go now. Okay, before we go much further, consider this formal service of our complaint regarding you and your teacher, a Mr. Henkel, for violating school policy as well as state law. My son Greydan could have lost his life yesterday due to you and your teacher's incompetence. Now, you further humili-ate this fine school by punishing the one person involved who was thinking and by his quick actions, managed to save Greydan's life?"

"What Ricky... Mr. Sayer? This is the first I have heard of this. I was told that Greydan had a bloody nose, and JoeJoe took him off of school property instead of to the school nurse. Further, I was told that his friends blatantly refused to listen to Mr. Henkel when they were told to go to the office after JoeJoe started a fight with a smaller boy in the lunch-room. Sit and tell me what you're talking about, please," begs the now contrite vice-principal as he motions with one hand to the chairs in front of his desk.

JoeJoe sits, then retells a concise, front-row-seat version of the events, to the ever more penitent Mr. Owens.

After JoeJoe's summary, Ricky Sayer adds, "The doctor stated in this deposition," the lawyer hands a piece of paper to the shrinking vice-principal, "that when the Donny White boy hit my son, it caused a cut in an artery. Had his brother and his friends not acted as quickly as they did, he would have likely died. Harry, Lucy is just now getting home from the hospital with our son. Now, what I'd like to know is where was Mr. Henkel when JoeJoe was being bullied, and Greydan was hit. I know you understand that a lot of smaller kids and even some men like to make a big name for themselves by beating up on the bigger guys. Since you're a big guy yourself, and we went to this very school together, I do know how you were treated."

"Yes, Ricky, you're right. JoeJoe, you can go back to class. If I need you, will you mind speaking with the other boy present?" the vice-principal asks.

"I don't mind, Sir. Bye, Dad, and thank you." JoeJoe shakes hands with his dad and the lawyer who's standing silently. He leaves just in time for the lunch bell.

JoeJoe makes it there ahead of the others and buys lunch the way he does most of the time. He sees Donny White smirk at him and starts in his direction. Then in perfect synchronicity with the wheels of justice, the overhead speakers crackle once again. "Donny White, you're needed in the vice principal's office immediately."

Donny's face loses all color, and he pivots on one foot, leaving the cafeteria and passing near enough to Jana, Asa, and Kaden that he has to shift his path to avoid them. They make their way to JoeJoe ... and food. Asa sits down and plows into the food letting the big guy tell the others what happened. They all take it differently but are glad that it turned out well. Jana, ever the protector, wants to make sure someone is with the bigger guys at all times. The guys grin at her suggestion. But, it'll be like everything else, they'll let her have her way.

"Oh, before I forget, meet me in the parking lot as soon as you can after the bell. So, we can go check on Greyd," Jana reminds them.

17

IT IS SERIOUS

*S*itting in Greydan's room, the whole group of teens are happy and smiling to see that Greyd is fine. His face is swollen and bruised, he's moving much slower than they are used to seeing him. He's dressed and sitting on his bed with them and says, "I can go to school tomorrow, but I can't practice with the football team. The doctors gave me an exemption slip to give to Coach Perini.

JoeJoe says, "Just take it easy, and we will be watching out for you, too. Just in case a sawed-off lightweight picks on you!"

They all laugh and proceed to tell him about the conversations each of them had with Mrs. Scott, their principal, Mr. Owens—the vice principal, and even the police, regarding the attack on Greyd. Greydan laughs when JoeJoe tells about the confrontation between their dad and Mr. Owens. JoeJoe uses his best imitation of his dad's voice. There has never been a doubt in their minds concerning the influence their father has in the community. The way he had slapped down the vice-principal was something to marvel at for the group.

"I knew Mr. Owens is a little nuts, but it was epic when I

was able to shush him while I called dad to come help."
JoeJoe was laughing as he held up his finger like he had done
to the vice-principal.

"Yeah, Mr. Owens even looks so old. He's totally bald and
wrinkly. Your dad only has a touch of gray! I can't believe
they knew each other in school! I thought your dad was way
younger," adds a smiling Jana.

"At least we found out that the vice principal can be a
reasonable guy ... when he has to be," Asa states.

The conversation seems to be winding down, so Greydan
suggests, "Let's go down to the kitchen and get something."

As Jana nears his mirrored dresser, she smells the same
flower smell that she remembers from the diner bathroom.
She stops, then searches the side of the mirror. Asa is immediately at her side. He cocks his head, concentrating.

Kaden, seeing his two friends pause as abruptly as they
did, starts to say something, but Asa quickly quiets him by
holding up a hand. For Asa to do this to one of his friends
isn't a big deal. They know each other so well and trust each
other so entirely that Kaden doesn't take insult from the
gesture and waits for his friend to speak. Asa, still listening
says, "I could hear crying coming from the mirror ... and
then nothing." He turns and looks at Kaden a sharp look of
surprise on his face.

Jana says, "Yes, it's time we escalate this rescue. I was
given a book today from Mr. Janes that just might help. I'll
read it before I go to sleep and see if I can find something. I'll
let you all know." That's when her phone chimes, and she
looks at her messages. "It's detective Walsh asking if I can
meet him downtown at the courthouse in thirty minutes.
Asa, can you and Kaden go with me? I don't want to go by
myself, and I have a feeling I'll need both of your help."

"Yes, afterward, I need to go home and check to see that
my house is still standing," says Asa.

Kaden also answers, "Yep, I'll go home when my dad does. I'm doing as much research as I can on the mirror phenomenon. How about we try to plan the rescue this weekend, depending on if we have enough information to go safely?" They all agree.

As the three leave, JoeJoe hands them a bottle of water to take. Jana kisses him and Greyd before taking Asa and Kaden by the hand and walking out of the house.

JoeJoe and Greydan sit at the table, pawing through research of their own, while Chela, makes them some sandwiches and fawns over Greydan. She hands him a bag of frozen peas and says, "Put this on your nose. I'll get your medicines the doctor sent home." He holds the frozen vegetables on his nose as she reads and dispenses the appropriate medication from each of the bottles. He takes the meds from her and swallows them one at a time, trying to not make his face hurt any more than it does already.

"Greydan, mijo, I'm making you only soft food until you get better. Okay?" Chela asks.

Greydan looks at her with a bit of surprise. Chela has taken care of him and JoeJoe since they were young. She's always been kind of strict on them, making sure they live by whatever rules Mr. and Mrs. Sayer have put in place. Seeing her like this is unusual to the extreme. Are those tears in her eyes?

"Yes, ma'am. Thank you very much. You always cook good meals, I know I'll love whatever you make!" At this point, Greydan isn't going to look a gift horse in the mouth, enchiladas are soft!

Greydan's phone, set to vibrate, buzzes and moves around on the table. He picks it up and checks the caller ID and answers, "Hey, dad, what's up?"

"Greydan, I'm here with your vice-principal Owens. He

needs to hear your version of the attack if you don't mind. I have you on speaker," Mr. Sayer says.

"No, I don't mind," answers the now focused Greydan. He tells the whole story, including the part where he moved in front of JoeJoe to stop Donny from picking on his brother. JoeJoe had told his part earlier. The vice-principal is satisfied and thanks him.

"Boys, I'll see you at dinner. Thank you for your time and for being honest in your answers," concludes Mr. Sayer.

That night at dinner, Ricky has some news to tell his family. "I don't want this to become town gossip, but I need you to know what happened today. I already know you both will tell your friends, and that's okay. Just don't spread it around or make fun out of the situation please."

Lucy Sayer says, "You know we won't, hun. Just tell us how the situation was resolved. I don't want the boys to have to worry about this same kind of trouble again."

Taking a deep breath, Ricky presses on, "The White boy was arrested on charges of assault. He was also expelled from the school. He'll eventually have to face a judge, but for now, was released into his parents' care. Who I might add, don't believe he did anything wrong. They said he was acting on orders from someone else who had threatened his life if he didn't beat one of you up. No one knows who threatened him, and he says he's too scared to name names. Also, your football coach knows you can't be jarred around for a week or two. But Greydan, I still want you to take it easy for a while, please."

JoeJoe says, "I wonder why Mr. Henkel said I started the fight, Dad? Did anyone clear that up?"

"Now that's interesting, too. Two of the older lunch ladies interviewed said that Mr. Henkel wasn't even in the lunchroom when the fight broke out. He was actually in the pantry with one of the younger servers. I'll let you figure that out later. Presumably, he'd grilled Donny White and just parroted his story as if he had been a witness. Needless to say, when Harry confronted him about his activities in the pantry, he repeatedly attempted to deny it. Eventually, he came clean in hopes of saving his job. It didn't work. He was fired on the spot. I'm guessing he'll be hard pressed to find a teaching job around here again."

"Ricky, did you put pressure on the school to fire him, or anything like that?" Mrs. Sayer asks with an iron tone.

"No, Lucy, I didn't say a word. I even asked Harry if it were necessary to fire Henkel. Harry was very clear that this behavior is clearly outlined in the school policy manual. There is nothing the boys said, or I said which caused him to lose his job. As far as getting another job. There seems to be some sort of animus between Harry and the Henkel fellow which is the root of that." Ricky pauses to take a drink of his evening decaffeinated tea.

JoeJoe takes this pause as a chance to interject. "I was wondering why he hated me so much that he'd lie about what happened. Then it turns out it isn't even about me. It's about him covering up his own crap conduct."

Lucy pipes up, "That's usually the case in situations like this, son. More often than not, it's about the person trying to cover some personal failure or weakness of their own and not others. No matter what we might think, people act according to their own self-interests. Their anger, hatred or even envy is almost always more about their own personal issues than anything else. Now you two go get ready for bed, and if you have homework get it done before bed. Greydan, you need to go to school tomorrow, and, JoeJoe, I mean sleep, not just lay there."

The boys smile at their mom and get up and do just what she says.

18

THE JOB

*A*fter leaving the Sayers, Jana, Asa, and Kaden meet Kaden's dad in front of the courthouse and walk with him to see the DA. Just inside the atrium of the large offices, a tall, slender man with ebony black hair meets the group. He welcomes the detective with a handshake before turning to look dismissively at the three teens.

"District Attorney Forni, this is the team of teens I've been telling you about. They're known to have helped several townspeople, using their psychic abilities. They've volunteered to assist us in the Perrin case. They came forward to us because Miss Perrin was a classmate who they knew. Because of the unusual nature of their gifts, I wanted them to meet you first," says Detective Henry Walsh. He then turns to introduce each of the team. "This is Jana Jay…"

The tall DA rolls his eyes then sucks in a breath and interrupts the detective. "I'm sorry, Detective Walsh. However, I'm late for a meeting with the mayor. If you don't mind, the introductions will need to wait." Then turning to the team, he adds, "Thank you for volunteering, but if you're able to give us any information that leads to an arrest we have a special fund set up that we will give you an award from." He tries to cover his rude interruption by sounding more upbeat. It doesn't work.

The teens keep their faces blank. They know a canned speech if they ever heard one. Even the detective is amazed at the lack of respect. He covers the insult by saying, "Well, Forni, we're going to the murder site, and if they say anything actionable, I'll be back to get a search warrant going. I'll see you in a little while."

THE KIDS and detective arrive at the scene of the murder less than thirty minutes later. As they exit the car, they stand quiet and still for a few minutes. Kaden takes Jana's hand, and the teens wait until she indicates she's ready. Her shoulders relax, and she nods to the boys. They cross the road heading toward the truck stop rest area where Stacy's body was found.

Jana stops Kaden with a hand on his arm and says, "Please don't let your dad see what happens to me after a vision. I can feel the tingle beginning now. Just get me to the car or something, even if you have to carry me?" she pleads.

"Asa and I will take care of you," Kaden says and tightens his grip on her hand.

Detective Walsh watches them from a cement table by a vending machine. He told them earlier that he would let them look, and they could come to him with any further information that they might find, but even if they didn't figure out more than what they had told him before it was enough for him to get the warrant going.

The teens continue their walking tour of the site and are

now a little behind the bathrooms. Here, Jana notices a piece of something on the ground. She picks it up and hands it to Kaden. It looks like half of a butterfly hair clip. It might be nothing, but Jana has a feeling it's essential. She takes a step forward and says, "Oh, oh, I feel it coming, Kaden!"

Jana wobbles, getting her balance, feeling as if she just opened her eyes in a different time. She's in the same place, but it's different. It's dark, and a cold breeze is blowing. Jana shivers when she recognizes Stacy's spirit beside her, pouting, head hanging down, her arm is outstretched, and index finger pointing. Jana's vision enables her to see the ghost. Usually, only Greydan can see them unless the spirit has a lot of reason and power to be seen by the living.

Jana does as instructed and looks in the direction Stacy indicates. In front of her, the 'living' Stacy runs across the small field. She's panicked and scared as she hides behind the rest stop's bathrooms. Tears stain her pretty face. Jana listens as Stacy berates herself saying, "You're so stupid! Why do you always have to make yourself look like a fool?"

A shadow covers her. Jana moves closer. Standing by Stacy, arms raised high in the air, is the homeless man who Jana knows committed the murder. He strikes Stacy on the head with a large piece of wood smashing her skull. Stacy falls over, now a bloody heap at his feet. She was killed instantly. Again, and again, the vagrant raises the board, then pounds it into Stacy's head.

As he hits her, he's talking to himself saying, "Have to make sure she's dead."

Part of her butterfly hair clip is smashed into her temple, leaving its imprint. It also imprints onto the board used to kill her.

The tramp throws dirt on his board in an attempt to clean the blood off of it. He gets dirt on Stacy, too. He bends and takes her rings. Finally, he retrieves the purse that's lying on the ground near her and places it in an inside pocket of his long coat. Then he kicks her leg, moving it over the other one to cross them.

Satisfied at her grizzly pose, he leaves. Jana glances at spirit Stacy. She points after the man. Jana follows him. He stops in a nearby wood where he has a tent. It stinks of urine and feces. Here she watches as he lies down with his board and falls asleep.

Jana's body is on fire and shaking uncontrollably. The vision is over. Kaden holds her close to his chest. He tells her he'll take care of her and she's okay. Asa is behind her, they are pressed together tightly.

She moans, "Ummm, let me just touch you. You feel so good. Please." She groans into Kaden's neck kissing him and giving him little bites while she pushes her butt into Asa and puts a hand on his package.

Asa pleads, "Oh, God, please help. I wish this was private or she had control. I don't want to stop. Kaden, help."

Kaden forces himself to look up and see where his dad is and if he can see them. He's sure that they can't be seen right now, and they'll have a minute to calm their girl. He says calmly, "Jana, you have to come back, sugar." He shoves her tighter against Asa hoping if anyone comes up, they'll think it's a group hug.

Jana takes it as a sign and grinds even harder on Asa. Asa holds steady staring at his buddy, blinking and thinking of revenge. Kaden kisses her deeply, playing for time. His mind is racing, his hormones raging, but he has an idea. She had once blown in his mouth, teasing him during a kiss. They both thought it was hilarious and laughed quite a bit afterward. Kaden has to try something, so he takes a chance and blows in her mouth. Her cheeks puff out, and she stops moving and moaning and laughs out loud. Her energy now turns to laughter, and she cackles out.

As she leans backs into Asa, she cocks her head and watches his stunned look and laughs even harder. By now, Kaden is laughing. Asa knows what they are thinking but doesn't see the humor. He huffs, swinging out both arms and says, "You two are going to kill me."

That's how detective Walsh finds them when he walks around the corner of the bathrooms to check on them. Watching at the group with a 'what the hell have I gotten into' look, he asks, "Well, did you get a feeling or whatever it is you do?"

Jana, still captive of the passionate throb of her body, has a difficult time explaining what she saw. Since Asa knows, he tells the detective the story as Kaden hands him the half of the butterfly hair clip.

Detective Walsh's eyes are as big as saucers as the story ends and he takes the clip. The passion retreats, and remembering the horror, Jana adds that she saw where the homeless man lives. "It smells heavily of urine and feces. He has the board in his tent. He keeps it with him in the woods."

Kaden's father says, "I have more than enough to give to the DA for the warrant, kids. I want to thank you, Jana and boys, for what you've done, too. If no one else ever believes you, I do and always will. Go home now and get some food. Son, I'll be there in about an hour. Tell mom to not wait for dinner. I can heat mine up.

The teens all head back to their vehicles. Jana stands by Kaden and kisses him goodbye beside his car looking into his sparkling cognac eyes, she says, "Thank you for making me laugh, so I didn't embarrass us. I can't wait until we can be together that way. You're so hot I want you even without the vision heat."

Kaden answers breathily, "I'll be waiting for that day, too. But you're hotter than me, sug. I'll see you in the morning, okay?"

Walking away from her tall, muscular ballplayer wasn't easy, but she had her Elf Boy to take her home. She tears herself away and makes it to her own car and Asa. Asa drives them to her house where her parents are making a big pot of spaghetti. Since they make the best pasta, the two teens are happy to help with the garlic bread.

While they sit together as a family and eat, Jana tells the story of what happened at school concerning Greydan and JoeJoe and how Donny White was arrested then adds the part about Mr. Henkel being fired.

Nichole says, "Jana, I feel so bad that you all have to go through things like that, especially that Greydan is hurt. I'm glad you're all okay and learning, though. You all handled that situation well. I'm not sure I could have done better. Maybe, you would consider moving to the big city with us. Not trying to change the subject, but what is happening with the murder? You said you were going to help the police. Were you able to feel anything psychically and help with the case at all? I know all of you have gifts. It's been a while since we've discussed it, so I think you must have it under control and are at least happy with what you're doing. Am I right?"

Jana answers, "Yes, Mom, it's something that we just don't talk about much, except with each other. Most people are afraid of us unless they need help. We're okay with that, but we don't advertise our gifts. Concerning the murder ... I think all of us helped, and they're going to be able to solve it soon."

Jana's mom responds, "Well, I think you're all amazing. Asa, do you want more? There is plenty here." She fills his plate before he can answer.

Afterward, when the kitchen's cleaned, Jana and Asa

wander off to the playroom and sit on the sofa and read. Asa's phone rings. It's his boss. The shoot he's scheduled for on Saturday is canceled. He isn't hurt or even bothered. Asa says, "It's just more time for us." Jana is leaning against him, under his arm when they fall asleep, reading.

19

DEVELOPING THE PLAN

*J*ana wakes up in her own bed upstairs, remembering that she conked out on her boyfriend makes her smile. She's wondering why he didn't just let her stay asleep with him in the play-room. She'll ask him later, but for now, she has a lot to do to get started on her day. Uh oh, she forgot to text her guys and tell them what happened when she went to help in a psychic capacity for the DA. She wonders if Kaden or Asa texted them. They've been a group for so long that they all take up slack for each other. They think very much alike, and it sometimes happens without a second thought. If no one has shared the information from last evening, she'll tell them at lunch later.

Last night, she finished the book that Mr. Janes had given her in class. She didn't learn much from it, but what she did learn is important. When they put together what each of them has learned about mirrors and the supernatural, she's sure it will be enough to perform a safe rescue of the ones that they're convinced are being held prisoner inside the mirrors. Jana feels a desire to look in her mirror now to see if there's a hint there, but she resists. She might get caught up, and if there's trouble … but the pull is real.

When Jana is dressed, she walks downstairs. Everyone looks up at her like she has a spider on her head.

"What? Do I look okay?" she asks.

"Well, hun, did you look in the mirror at all this morning? Your ponytail is almost on the side of your head a little eighties style. Did you do that on purpose? If you did that's all right; no matter what, you're always beautiful to me," says Jana's mom Nichole with a quirky smile.

"What no, I mean yes, I guess I was just in a hurry this morning. Will you fix it, please?" Jana responds.

Of course, Asa and her dad keep quiet. Asa doesn't talk a lot, and her dad knows it'll not go well if he comments. So … the kitchen remains quiet. That is until dad asks, "Dear, would you like some breakfast, or do you want me to pop some toast down for you?"

Asa hands her some coffee just the way she likes it when she answers, "I'd love some toast with butter, dad."

When Jana and Asa are on the way to school, he says, "Hun, I know that you aren't looking in the mirror and why. Do you want me to come up when you're getting ready tomorrow, just to be sure you're safe? After you've dressed … of course."

"That'd be great. I've been avoiding looking in them all, but I do need to when I get dressed. We've got to get this job done, so I'm not afraid to use a stupid mirror. I don't want to have side ponytails again!" she answers. They both laugh at the small joke. "Asa, is there a reason that you took me upstairs to bed instead of cuddling with me last night?"

He swallows thickly before he says, "Honey, you tempt me so badly that I don't want to stop touching you. After the thoughts you had at the rest stop, I was so turned on that in no way would I be able to hold back last night. I'm better today and can control myself and won't keep from touching you unless you ask."

Jana smiles and cuddles close to him for the rest of the ride to school. When they arrive, they meet the others in the parking lot. "I'm sorry, I forgot to text you last night to let you know what happened. I got caught up in a book and fell asleep on the couch. I promise to tell you everything at lunch."

They all let her know it's okay.

Greydan says, "Kaden managed to let us know the details last night, so we weren't worried, or we would've called. We knew you were safe with Asa, anyway, since he's staying at your house until the murderer is arrested."

"Are you sure you should be here today, Greyd? Your face looks really hurt," Jana asks.

"The doctors cleared me for everything except football, baby. I'll be careful, but you can help me walk if you want. I feel like I need your help." Greyd wobbles a little as he says that and has a sly grin that makes the others laugh.

Jana walks up and tucks herself under his arm and says, "You poor baby, let me help you." She laughs too.

Later when they meet at lunch, the cafeteria grows very quiet when Greyd enters. He waves his hand around to everyone and says, "Hey, guys, it's okay. I'll be football ready in no time." A small round of laughter and some cheers end the silence, and the general low roar of the cafeteria returns as things get back to normal.

Jana starts to tell the boys all about the book that she read. The one about the supernatural things connected to mirrors. "It seems that mirrors are portals. Sort of the way we thought that it was a hallway to another realm. It might be more of a way to get to another world for sure. The book suggests that we might have to anchor to our realm before we go. We will also need to carry sage or sweetgrass and maybe even onyx. The onyx can also be used as a mirror … just a darker one. The author's sure there's a difference between the lighter and darker mirror portals. He described them in a religious or witchcraft type sense with a general preference to the lighter choice of the religious.

"I think we should be as neutral as possible, even though we spent our primary grades in St. Augustine's. I still want to cover all our bases. What do you guys think about trying to ask the Creator for protection and see if he's in the realm of the mirrors or knows about them?"

Jana is speaking of a spirit who introduced himself as the Creator when they were very young. He has always helped them when they have especially hard things to accomplish in the spirit realm. When they have a dangerous or possibly unsafe situation, he sometimes helps. Sometimes, he sends angels to help them through a sticky situation. They aren't the cutesy cupid types, either. They're large warrior types … and absolutely scary. When the Creator or the angels tell demons what to do, they do it. But usually, the evil spirits try to leave as soon as they notice them. Now, that they are older and don't take much for granted, they have thought they should get to know this Creator spirit more and maybe find out who he is and where he comes from.

They all agree and set it as an agenda item for tomorrow after school. Fortunately, for this plan at least, the football game is out of town, and Greyd can't go, much less play. That means none of them are going, either. They'll have all day without any worry about needing to be any place in particular.

"It's time we help the prisoners in the mirror realm. We'll

meet at Greyd's and summon the Creator in the boathouse like we've done in the past," Jana says. They don't answer. They don't need to, after being together so long, she knows they agree with her.

Without any warning or context, her mind jumps to next week's Fall Formal. *Ooohhh, we need to get ready for this, too!*

20

SUMMONING THE CREATOR

*N*ow that the school day's over, all the teens stretch out on the furniture in the Sayers' boathouse. They have the snacks that Chela made for them piled inside their little circle. Well, they aren't sure if they could consider a tamale a snack. Ultimately, Asa decides it has to be, or Chela wouldn't have made it for them. So … they can have more than one. That the little cook told them, "Only one each, you can have more at dinner," was conveniently forgotten.

Jana said, "Are we ready for the summoning ceremony, guys?" They had made up a ceremony as children and were shocked when it worked. They haven't changed any part since that time.

A murmur of assent rolls around the room. They each adjust their position on the floor until they form a circle with their knees touching. "Okay let's begin. She places a well-used and large candle in the center of their group. The candle is one they had poured themselves. It's obviously handmade and has six different wicks; five circling one slightly larger wick in the center. Without prompting, each of them draws out a long matchstick and lights the wick nearest them.

Together, they chant, "This lighting represents my individuality and my gift."

After this, they join their matches at the center wick. It lights. Again, they chant, "This lighting represents the joining of my individuality and my gift. We bond as one."

By now, none of them have their eyes open, and they're each breathing deeply. They reach for each other's hands and hold on.

Jana says a short prayer out loud, "Creator, we've joined together as one. Together we call you. Creator, come and help us."

The boathouse fills with an airy mist. The haze dancing within the candlelight forms a double rainbow circling the inside the boundary of the room. A scent of spices perfumes the air. The teens are immersed in a deep trance when a familiar voice calls out to them.

"Hello, Oracle. Hello, my children."

They've seen and heard this spirit dozens of times over the years. When they were younger, they would often speak to this spirit to learn about their gifts and how to use them. As they mature, they speak less often, but in greater depth. They all hear the Creator speak and look over at him.

Jana breaks the silence and asks, "Creator, will you help us? We've found prisoners who we're trying to rescue from a place that can only be reached from a mirror. It looks like an infinity mirror. When I touched it, my fingers sank in. A being there ... something that's trapping the others stole part of me. I couldn't move until the boys tricked the thing into giving it back to me."

"I'll help you, Oracle, but you need to know that this is not a realm per se but a doorway to another world. The one in charge there is called Dorn, he's a dark magic user. I'll do what I can to keep you safe, but stay away from Dorn. He's very powerful. Avoid him at all costs." Then pausing briefly before he continues in an obviously curious tone he asks, "Oracle, why would you desire to assist these prisoners? You don't even know them."

"We felt the prisoners, and they're miserable. We don't want anyone to be held this way. We enjoy using our gifts to help others. We're sure we can help these them. But we thought it might be dangerous. That's why we called you, for protection. Also, my name's Jana, not Oracle. I thought you knew that. I'm not trying to be rude, but why would you call me Oracle instead of Jana?"

The spirit grows, and his voice changes from conversational to deep and authoritative. "Jana, you are an oracle, I named you by your title. You are my Oracle. Why do you think I've been sending you visions all these years?"

Jana is surprised but not. She pauses then nods her head accepting the truth of this statement before saying, "I see that's true. I hadn't figured it out until now. We want to get to know more about you. Do you have any other name besides … Creator?"

"I'm called by many names, Eros is among them, do you like it better? Do you want to use it instead of Creator?" He asks as his tone returns to informal.

Again, it's Jana who answers, "Yes, I would. I like Eros better."

Eros continues, "I understand that you have a desire to help others. That's why I choose to answer you when you call to me. You serve something greater than yourselves. I'll give you protection when you go against Dorn."

"Thank you. What do we need to do?"

"Stand silently until I am finished."

All of the teens stand and stay still in the circle holding hands. A heavy mist falls over them, covering them like warm honey until they're completely covered. The feeling is comforting.

"You can sit back down now. Tell me when do you plan to go on this mission?"

"We're planning to go tomorrow. Eros ... isn't that the Greek god of love's name?" asks Jana.

"Yes, it is, but I'm not who people think of when they think of Eros today. I was there at the founding of this world. I was the only male when Gaea and Chaos, both being female, needed a male so that they could bear children and shape the world. And yes, I've been connected to you since your birth. I've tried to watch over all of you, but I'm limited. I don't live on Earth. I live on the wind, and like you. I like to help others. Oracle, my time here is up. You can call on me again. If I don't hear, Aether will tell me, she is my friend and everywhere. Just give me time I can't do everything instantly or on a whim. There are laws to which even I must adhere."

With that, he's gone. The release on Jana is instant. She rises, almost too excited. The burst of talking is immediate and loud. Their excitement is so high that they are speaking over one another.

Jana stops. Her hand slaps over her wide-open mouth as she stares directly at Greydan. The others stop talking and their eyes move first from Jana, and the shock on her face to Greyd. "Wow, would you look at that!" Jana squeals. Kaden, Asa, and JoeJoe's eyes go wide and their jaws slack.

JoeJoe is the first to speak, "What in the holy hell happened to your face?"

Greydan goes slack-jawed himself. "What is it? What happened? Did I turn into Erebos?" They all laugh, thinking of the mythology of the monster who wanted Andromeda in the Clash of the Titan's movie.

"You're so weird! No, but that is funny considering we

just learned that Eros is who we've been calling the Creator," says Kaden.

"No, Greyd, your face is totally healed!" Jana exclaims.

"Jana how are we ever going to tell people how he healed up?" Asa asks quizzically.

Jana moves over to inspect Greyd's face up close.

The blue-eyed jock blinks and says, "What should we say for cover?"

"Maybe we can just say it's makeup that Jana put on you because you got tired of people feeling sorry for you," says JoeJoe, punching his brother in the arm.

Jana finishes her big beau's point for him. "Let's go with that for now. Use it if anyone asks, otherwise let's avoid going around people for a few days."

JoeJoe adds, "If it gets too bad, Kaden, you'll have to use your gift to make others think it's natural."

Kaden says, "Yeah, I can do that. So, concerning going into the mirror are we really doing that tomorrow?"

"What do you think, Greyd? Are you okay with it or does anyone have a bad feeling?" Kaden asks.

The group of kids check to sense the depth of them. This little routine has served them well in the past. They've learned not to ignore a lousy gut reaction and tend to evaluate if it could be just pure personal fear, or a warning from somewhere. They have believed for a long time that this is an unused part of natural human senses which most people ignore as impossible.

"No, no bad feelings I just want to be sure that we're all in and good with this. The sooner, the better especially since Eros just gave us a protective covering. I have to ask, did any of you feel like you were being covered in goo at first?" Greydan laughs.

"That pretty much describes what I thought," Jana quips.

All the teens agree and are sure they're protected. "I definitely want to stay for dinner and more of Chela's tamales. Is everyone going to stay the night here tonight? Do you need to ask your parents if it's all right?" asks Asa facing Greyd and JoeJoe.

"No, they haven't made us ask in years, but we do like to tell them so that they know and plan for it just in case they have plans, too. JoeJoe come with me while I ask, will you?" Greydan asks.

"Okay, but you do the talking and keep your face hidden if at all possible. I don't want mom asking a ton of questions. They would never believe the truth." With that, the brothers walk off toward the house, and the three left decide to play a board game until they get back.

Kaden hands them all a mouthpiece from a game called Speak Out. When they play this, the rules are a little different. Since Asa can read the mind of people in the room, he can speak with the mouthpiece when it is his turn, but he is forbidden to guess. He tries to block out the thoughts of the other players and is really good at it. But he still feels enough from them that his guesses are always correct. He's good with playing this way, anyway.

The game is pretty simple. You each have a mouthpiece that you place in your mouth then when it's your turn, you read a card. The mouthpiece severely distorts the shape of your mouth and your words as you try to pronounce them clearly, so the other players can guess what you are saying. The first person to guess wins the card. The person with the most cards at the end of the game wins.

Kaden places his mouthpiece in to start the game. Let me describe the mouthpiece properly. What it looks like installed in your face is well ... imagine ... you're at the dentist, and she wants to literally erase your lips, so she has complete access to your teeth. Got it? You've got no lips! Oh, and to make it even better, this thing in your mouth ...

there's a reason your mom told you not to talk with food in there. Besides spitting food everywhere, you're freaking hard to understand. Anyway, you cut it, with this thing in your mouth, you look like a crazy person. A crazy person who just had their first retainer installed while their pet gerbil is biting a nipple off. On top of it all, you now sound like a five-year-old with an inverted lisp.

So, the handsome, brown-eyed Kaden erases his lips and dramatically draws the first card. His dramatics combined with no lips and the odd look on his face as he sees the card has Jana falling over laughing, just looking at him. His reading of the card threatens to send her into hysterics, "hhheees I ellhee het herret name arrett."

Jana is usually pretty good at this game, but her laughing sometimes makes it hard for her to guess. She's worked her way through most of it after several tries … "Okay, you're saying 'He is my stealthy pet parrot named Garrett', right?

"No! 'herrett! herrett! herrett!' You know like a scirl!" By now Kaden is drooling and trying to clean it with a paper towel … and failing. He's also saying his words louder as if it'll help them understand it better.

Jana and Asa are laughing so hard at the utter exasperation on Kaden's face when Jana finally gets it. "He is my stealthy pet ferret named Garett!" she screams joyfully.

Relieved, Kaden removes his mouthpiece and says, "Yes!" Before falling, exhausted, onto the couch with Jana.

She looks at him, still laughing, she asks, "Handsome, oh, my stars and garters, what is a 'scirl'?"

"I was trying to tell you it looks like a 'squirrel!' I guess it came out worse than ferret. Didn't it?" answers Kaden as he rubbed his jaws from the mouthpiece but mainly from laughing.

Asa is reading a card, and the three are still laughing uncontrollably when JoeJoe and Greyd return.

JoeJoe says, "Well they never even looked at us, so they didn't even notice Greyd's face. They're busy packing. Dad's got an emergency trip to England for the company, and mom's going with him. Their plane leaves in a few hours. They only said don't burn the house down and watch over Greydan. It's time to go in, though, Chela has dinner ready."

Dinner is fantastic, as always, and the teens stuff themselves on the little cook's Mexican food. Afterward, they go into the movie room and are deciding on a movie, but the conversation turns to the mirror. Jana reminds them it's really a portal.

"Kaden says, "That makes sense because Eros said it's a doorway. I guess we'll see where it leads to tomorrow."

Jana adds, "The book also says we need to anchor ourselves to this world before we go so that we don't get lost. I'm not sure what that means. Should we look it up?"

"Good idea, sugar. Phones or computer?" Kaden asks

They take their phones out and start Googling then calling out information to each other. By the end of the hour, they have a clear plan and begin the movie.

Ricky and Lucy Sayer come in, and they stop the flick, so they can give hugs and say goodbye. "We will be home in a week," Ricky says.

As Lucy is hugging Jana, she tells her, "I'll find you each something nice while I'm there." Kaden does have to use his gift when Lucy notices that Greyd is healed. Then she says, "I'm not going to try to figure out how you got better so fast. But I do feel better about leaving."

21

ALWAYS TOGETHER

That night while Jana and her guys are in Greydan's ample room trying to sleep, they begin to talk instead. Jana's laying on the bed next to Greydan with Asa on her other side, being his usual quiet self. JoeJoe's on a large futon, and finally, Kaden's on the chaise part of the sofa. JoeJoe's bedroom is the same size, but the teens never really go in there. They never talked about choosing one room over the other. It's something they just did.

Greydan asks, "Jana did you think when Eros said that you're 'his oracle,' it answered a bunch of questions we've had over the years. Like why you always need to be touched and want sex after a vision. He is the god of love after all. He even said he was, and also if he was there with the Earth mother Gaea and Chaos that would affect a lot. I think that's why we were all brought together. It's a way to help you with that part of your gift. I'm kinda glad to know it, too. I always wondered what happened that made the visions do that to you."

JoeJoe says, "It really helps me to know that we didn't do anything wrong to cause the … you know … vision thing. I was afraid it was all our fault. Now I think it's fate, and I feel way better."

Kaden says in all seriousness, "I didn't know that any of the Greek gods were real. I wonder if all of them are?"

Asa snorts and laughs at the comment but says nothing, his hand rubbing softly on Jana's arm at his side.

Jana smiles and says, "It does answer a lot, doesn't it? I wonder why he is just now telling us. Do you think it has to do with our turning eighteen?"

Greydan says, "It wouldn't surprise me if that's the case. Did anyone think the protection thing did anything else to us? I felt like I was as close as we have ever been with all of you when it was over."

They all agree that they had a similar feeling, but since they're already very close, it isn't a big deal. The room quiets as dreams approach. But like most teens, this group fights to stay awake longer … to talk for a few more minutes.

Jana says, "Speaking of being close, I want to talk to you all about something. I know you don't like the girlie stuff, and I know that you all love me. But now that we are older and starting to make future decisions … I just want each of you to know how much I love you. But I don't want the decision we made as children … to stay together forever … to kinda force you to stay in this relationship. If you want out of it, I want you to have the choice. Does that make any sense?"

Asa says, "I don't do this often, honey, but I am going to speak for us all right now. We know we love you and you love us. There is no other girl that we want the way we want you. You know us inside and out and love us, anyway. You want us even though we're weird and damaged in various ways. We've been together for so many years, Jana, that to be without you would be like cutting off part of ourselves. We're going into this part of our lives with our eyes and hearts wide open. We're committed to you whether we've made a formal declaration or not.

Jana holds onto Greydan and Asa's hands. She has tears in her eyes when she says, "Thank you, that was something important for me to know. I won't ask again until I ask if you'll marry me, but that's going to wait for a long while if you're all okay with that." Then she says, "Hey, Kaden, did your dad say whether they were able to make an arrest or not?"

Kaden answers her, "I'm really okay with that, sugar. No, he never said if they did. I'm sure it would be in the news. Let me look online and see. If not, I'll ask him first thing in the morning." After a few minutes, he says, "I don't see a thing, and I'm sure that it would be reported if they've arrested him."

"Do you think the homeless guy is hiding from them?" Jana asks.

Again, Kaden answers her, "No telling, sug, they'll find him soon, even if he's hiding. They're good at their jobs, and if we need to, we'll just have to help them again."

Wanting to change the subject, so she can rest her mind and sleep, Kaden asks, "Want to play, 'Let's make up a story'? I'll start if you do. There was a pretty girl who was making a cake for her boyfriend's birthday ..."

JoeJoe picks up the story, "She thought she wanted to add some extra love into the recipe and asked a little fairy if she had some to add. The little fairy ..."

Asa continues, "Was really a troll in disguise and gave her a sleeping potion which the pretty girl used double the amount of in the cake, so it would be extra special ..."

Greydan adds, "That night after dinner the pretty girl brought the cake to the boy and sang "Happy Birthday" for him. She was so full of dinner, she decided to wait. But the guy was like Asa and was a bottomless pit. He took a giant piece of cake to make his girl happy …"

Now it is Jana's turn, she decides to end the story and go to sleep, so she says, "He falls fast asleep at the table with his face in his plate. The girl was sobbing with tears and grabs her cloak to find the evil little fairy who gave her the potion. When she finds the fairy, she kicks the troll's butt and holds it against the wall by the neck until it gives up the remedy. She runs home and pours it down her boyfriend's throat, and he wakes up smiling at her, never knowing anything was wrong."

Then Kaden says, "But it had a side effect and turned him into a troll. Yet, the pretty girl loved him anyway. Goodnight, Mary Ellen."

To which a sleepy yawning Jana replies, "Goodnight John Boy."

22

A CHALLENGE

*T*he teens wake up early the next day. While the guys take turns using Greydan's shower, Jana showers, and dresses in JoeJoe's room. This has been their modus operandi for several years. At least it's been this way since she developed a woman's body, anyway. They head down to eat breakfast together. Used to be, they would try to skip Sunday breakfast, but Chela had a big fit. They don't even consider trying that again.

While they're eating, Chela says, "Security is still here and will watch over you today, but today is the beginning of my weekend. I'm going to spend it with my daughter, Mary." She kisses each of them on the forehead and heads out the door shouting instructions to them about how to reach her as she walks away. They're alone. Well, that is except for the … you know armed guards who're watching from behind the scenes.

Kaden's phone rings. Like always, Kaden checks to see who's calling before he answers, "Hey, guys, it's my dad." The quartet quiets as he answers, "Hello, dad."

… There's a quiet space as Kaden waits on his dad to finish.

"Yes … Okay, dad."

"We thought that it was all taken care of."

"Well, that's good news!"

"Yeah, we will. Thanks, dad."

"I love you too, bye."

"You guys will never believe this. Dad just asked if we are all together and said for us to stay here that the homeless guy was seen earlier, and they have him trapped in a large fairly open area. He said they're working on finding him. They did find Stacy's rings and the board with her blood and the butterfly clip still stuck to it, in his tent."

As if saying her name calls her, the spirit of the dead girl shows up in front of them clear as day. She looks delighted and is smiling at them. Asa tells them, "She's ready to move on to the other side now. She wants to tell us 'thank you.' She's sure the police will catch the guy now. It's just a matter of hours, and she's decided she wants to go on. She's telling us goodbye."

"Stacy is there anything you want us to tell anyone for you?" Jana asks.

The spirit looks down then back up with a hopeful look then Asa says, "She says that she had a fight with her mom the day she died and said some things that she can't take back. She knows her mom thinks that she didn't love her, but it's far from true. She has a diary hidden under a loose brick in the backyard by her old playhouse. She'd like us to give it to her mom. It'll tell her just how much she loves her and her dad."

Jana says, "That's something we can do. I'll make sure that we do it soon, too, goodbye, Stacy." All of the boys follow and tell her goodbye also as she waves and fades from sight with a happy glow on her face.

They let the quiet set for a while, none of them wanting to be the one who breaks it. Kaden decides to break it first, "I wonder if any of that showed up on the monitors?"

Greydan tells them, "I doubt they would say anything if it did. People either disregard strange things like this, or ignore them. It's not something they like to bring up unless it's brought to them. They will try to be honest about what they saw if they think the person can grasp the idea of the truth, and maybe even believe them. If not, they'll explain it away and forget it happened."

"So, do you want to go get the diary then come back to release the mirror prisoners?" Jana asks her boys.

"Yes, let's do that. I've felt like we needed to do something since we didn't go to Stacy's funeral. This'll be just the thing," says JoeJoe. That's all it takes, and they're ready to go. Greydan tells security where they'll be before they take off in JoeJoe's big truck.

When they arrive at the Perrin's Large home, Jana is struck with the petty frustrations she and Stacy had gone through, not to mention how insignificant most of them seem to be in hindsight. The yard is well manicured and very open. The gate on the four-foot tall wrought iron fence isn't locked. While Jana and the other guys stand on the front porch, JoeJoe goes to the backyard to find the diary. He puts his hand on the fence and knows right where Stacy had hidden it. He quickly retrieves it and returns to the front porch with the others.

Jana rings the bell. It's opened by Stacy's dad, Jana notices that company must have recently arrived, as Mrs. Perrin is taking them to the sitting room. JoeJoe hands the little book to Kaden who is speaking. "Mr. and Mrs. Perrin, we wanted to offer our condolences for your loss." Kaden gives a little push of comfort to the grieving parents. They visibly relax and smile graciously in return. Kaden hands the book to Jana and gives her a small nod.

This is Jana's part. "Mrs. Perrin, we all knew Stacy, and she gave me her diary a few weeks ago. She told me she'd like you to have it so that you would know how much she loves you and Mr. Perrin." Just a little of the details left out, mostly true except for the time period. Jana crosses her fingers hoping Stacy's mom doesn't ask why she would give her the diary.

Mrs. Perrin sucks in a deep breath, gasping at Jana's words. Tears start down her cheeks as she asks, "Did she tell you that?"

Jana answers, "Yes, ma'am, she did."

Mrs. Perrin takes the little book from Jana with a quiet sound of sorrow breaking out even though she desperately wanted to hold it in. She was tired from the days of tears and the stress of losing a child. "Thank you, Jana. Thank you all. This is something I needed more than words can say. I'll always treasure it. You know, I didn't even know that Stacy had a diary. I can't thank you kids enough for stopping and making sure that we have this. Would you like some dessert? We have a lot of cake and brownies that our neighbors have brought us."

"No, but thank you, and you are very welcome. We knew you both would treasure this," Kaden said. Adding more comfort to his work, he added, "We have to be on our way now. We just needed to be sure that Stacy's last wishes were adhered to and are glad you're happy." Jana squints just a little, knowing that he added some extra magic to the last of that statement, so they'd work toward happiness.

After they're buckled in their seats, they pause letting the enormity of what they'd done wash over them. The joy they each feel at helping the Perrins provides a wellspring of happiness. Unknown to any of them, they'll need this reservoir to draw on soon.

"Let's go get something to drink then go let some prisoners go, okay, guys?" Jana requests.

23

AND THE HITS

*W*ith the door to Maize's Restaurant opening often with customers who have the same idea as Jana and her guys, the diner has taken on a chilly temp. Maize is in the cafe tonight and is regaling the teens with a story from her many years of dealing with people, as she makes their hot chocolate.

The door opens again, adding to the biting nip and nobody pays any particular attention until he yells, almost incoherently, "Everyone, put your hands up!" To make his point, he raises the large handgun he's holding and pokes it at Carol, the hostess.

Jana gasps, surprised at her instant recognition of Stacy's murderer standing just a few feet in front of her with a gun. Apparently, the guys also know precisely who he is as first JoeJoe, then the other three move to block Jana from the crazy murderer's line of sight. They form a protective ring around her so quickly the vagabond killer doesn't even notice them doing it.

Throughout the room, diners and employees raise their hands. Large numbers of them are able duck outdoors.

Employees in the kitchen drop down under cover of their cook stations, and many of them are also able to exit the building. The diner is built to hold fifty customers and another fifteen employees. While the building wasn't at capacity, it did contain a large percentage.

The lunatic hobo noticing the people escaping, fires a shot into the ceiling of the room and screams, "Nobody better move, or I'll … I'll start shooting yous!"

His words are odd, but his actions seem even more strange. Jana and the others have experience seeing this man on the streets. While he was never eloquent at speaking, they never heard him say 'yous.' Also, his words are fast and run together. He's sweating profusely, and they can smell his stink across the room. He is high on something for sure.

His laugh is crazed, and his movements aren't smooth. He is jerking and almost robotic. He moves to the counter close to the crew of teens and says, "All phones on the counter." To emphasize his point, he pushes JoeJoe, by far the biggest guy in the diner, with the end of his gun. The big guy complies and eyes Jana and the others, in effect telling them to do what the criminal says.

The vagrant murderer shouts, "Now put your monies in the bag." He thrusts a filthy pillowcase at JoeJoe to use before yelling at him, "Yous, go get it all and get what's in the register, too."

Jana's big boy takes the register money first then is halfway around the room when everyone hears sirens, loud and squalling. The homeless guy panics and grabs the bag from JoeJoe. Not satisfied with only taking the bag, he hits JoeJoe hard on his temple with the butt of the gun.

Jana freaks out and races forward to attack the asshole. Tears run freely down her face. Greydan catches her around the waist and restrains her. She's kicking and doing her best to get loose. Greydan holds her tight as the wacko leaves with the bag of money. When he's gone, Greyd lets his girl down. She runs to JoeJoe's side … Greydan runs with her. JoeJoe has a cut that looks awful, but on inspection, it's just a small cut with a big goose-egg and a lot of blood. Jana puts one of the cloth napkins on his head as the police enter the diner.

Several of the patrolmen take off when someone tells them the direction the homeless guy ran.

EMTs arrive almost as soon as the police. Since JoeJoe is the only injury and is still unconscious, they quickly move him to a stretcher and prepare him for travel to the local hospital. Within a few minutes, JoeJoe is coming around in the back of the ambulance. They are getting ready to leave, and the lead EMT says, "If any of you are family, one of you can go with him."

Immediately, Jana answers, "I'm his sister." She glances at her beaus who give her approving nods. Greyd's sure his brother is in good care. It's probably just a 'concussion and a couple of stitches' kind of emergency.

When the ambulance pulls away, Greydan calls his parents. They had only recently landed at Heathrow in London and are on their way to their hotel when Lucy Sayer answers her phone.

"Mom, I don't want you to worry. Everything's okay, but you need to know that JoeJoe got hurt and is on his way to the ER."

"What?" she shouts into the phone, then to her husband, "No, turn around, Ricky, we have to go home! It's JoeJoe, Greydan is telling me he's on the way to the ER." Then Lucy turns the conversation back to her son, "Now what happened. Is he awake? Is it terrible?" she asks in rapid fire.

"No, no, mom it's alright. You don't need to come home. It's just a couple of stitches. They might just put sterile-strips on it. He got hit on the head, but Jana is with him. I promise we have this under control."

"Okay, if you say so. I put you on speaker," Lucy says. Then again to her husband, she says, "It's okay, we don't have to go back. Go on to the hotel." Then back to her son, "Now, what happened, Greydan?" she asks.

He starts, then falters, trying to think of the best way to tell her then says, "Well …"

She quips shortly, "Greydan, now!"

He replies, "Okay, mom, but listen until I finish."

He can hear her reluctant, "Okay." He knows he has to do this well.

Greydan begins, "Jana remembered that she had Stacy Perrin's diary. Also, since we missed the funeral because I was in the ER, we decided to take it to her parents and give them our condolences at the same time. So, we told security where we were going and went. Mom, the Perrins were really appreciative, by the way."

Mom says, "Go on, Greyd."

He's glad she used his nickname that means she might be calmer when he continues, "After we finished, we decided to get some hot chocolate from Maize's before we went home. Here's what went wrong, a homeless guy came into the diner to rob the place at gunpoint …"

"That fucking rips it. Ricky, turn the car around!" Lucy shouts.

"Wait! Mom, you said you would wait until I finished. Dad, don't turn the car around. Let me finish. The homeless guy made us put our phones on the counter, so we couldn't call the cops. Then he gave a bag to JoeJoe and told him to get everyone's money including what's in the register. So, JoeJoe went to the register first. I'm sure he took the money that triggers the silent alarm. I don't know if I ever told you this, but Maize had shown us that alarm when it was installed."

"Greydan Sayer!"

"Sorry, mom. Anyway, the cops came after a minute or two. When he heard the sirens, the jerk homeless guy yanked the bag out of JoeJoe's hand and hit him on the temple with his gun. Then he ran. JoeJoe is fine really, mom."

Greydan notices that right beside him Asa is talking to Kaden who points to him and the phone. Greydan gets it and nods his head. Before his mom can wind up for another, 'we have to leave' rendition, Greyden says, "Mom, Kaden needs to talk to you a sec." He hands the phone to his friend and listens, hoping his friend's gift works through phones.

"Hello, Mr. and Mrs. Sayer. I wanted to let you know that your son is doing fine. He asked me to tell you 'hi' and said that he'll call you soon. He's just fine, please put your mind at ease. JoeJoe and Greydan are both safe, and we're going to stay the night again at your house with the security team. If anything at all happens, we'll be sure to call you ... quickly." There's a pause, and before he hangs up, Kaden answers, "Yes, ma'am, I will. Have a nice time in England." Handing the phone back to Greydan, he says, "We need to get JoeJoe to call them later." His eyes are wide, and he smiles, privately happy his gift works long distance.

Greydan nods and gives his friend a quick 'thanks for the help' smile. Then he catches sight of the growing crowd outside of the diner. Looking around, he also notices there are only a few people left inside the restaurant. Greydan, Kaden, and Asa walk to the door to see what everyone else is looking at. The police are loading, or are trying to load, the homeless guy into a patrol car. He's a little dirtier than he was before, but he looks just as crazy.

He's fighting the police, and they use several officers to subdue him. Somehow, he manages to break free. As he begins to run, an officer grabs him by the front of his shirt. The loon bites the cop on the wrist. Blood is gushing from the wound. The asshole knocks another of the policeman down, and he grabs his gun in the process. He's looking around wildly, his eyes alight with the fire of a bad drug high.

Not one of the cops takes the shot. They are still trying to reason with the guy, in the hopes of avoiding killing him. They are also worried about the safety of the people in the crowd. A stray bullet fired from a police weapon is just as deadly as a bullet from the lunatic's gun. The police warn the bum to hit the ground. There's no response except for crazy looks.

The homeless guy jerks his gaze from one direction to another when Asa yells, "Get down he's going to shoot into the crowd. He wants to commit suicide by cop."

Most of the crowd does drop down. As the drug-addled murderer turns his weapon toward the group, he is shot several times by the police, thereby getting his wish. It's a solemn moment for all of the onlookers. The crowd is stunned with the fast pace of the events. But the police aren't and move the crowd away and cordon off the area.

Afterward, the boys give statements. Kaden's dad who is also on the scene makes sure the boys are all right and asks about Jana and JoeJoe. After listening to them, he tells the boys, "I need you all to go home. There's nothing else you can do here."

"Dad, that's what we want to do. We're headed to the hospital to pick up Jana and JoeJoe. I promise I'll call you when we get to Greydan's house."

24

BROTHERS

The crew loading up into JoeJoe's truck without him is really strange. Greydan had been given a key to the truck by JoeJoe the day he got it new for his eighteenth birthday. JoeJoe had told him, "It's just in case you might need to use it. This way you don't need to ask." They decided JoeJoe was indeed a great guy ... and maybe even a bit prescient.

As they arrive in the parking lot of the hospital, Greydan's phone rings. It's Jana, she says, "We're finished. JoeJoe is okay. Can you guys come to pick us up? I'd like to get him home and in bed."

Greydan laughs a knowing laugh. "Baby, we just pulled up," Jana laughs her knowing laugh. It's bizarre how often the 'timing' of things works out for this group. They call it fate. After learning about Eros, it might really be Fate.

Greyd says, "We're on our way inside."

The doors slide open, and they find Jana sitting beside JoeJoe in the waiting area. JoeJoe glances up and smirks, getting up slowly with Jana's help. The others know he's going to ham it up to stay close to her for a while. Who can blame him? They would all take advantage of it, given a chance. Greyd walks over and looks over his brother. Seeing that he has had the injury pulled together with steri-strips and the blood washed off of his face, Greyd can easily see the bruise and the golf ball-sized goose-egg on the side of his head. His shirt is covered in dried blood, but that's all the remaining damage. He smiles at his big brother and asks with an ornery look, "Did they at least do an X-ray to make sure that that thick skull of yours didn't get cracked?"

"They did, and my thick skull is intact, thank you very much. Can we leave now?"

"Yep," answers Greydan.

"I expect you drove," wonders the injured boy.

"Yep, again!" says his brother.

"Do you mind still driving? I can't until after I see the doctor tomorrow and he says it's okay," adds JoeJoe.

"Ding, ding, ding. We have a 'Yep-tac-toe' winner!" The others laugh at the gentle banter between the brothers. "No problem. I'm glad you're okay. Is there any paperwork that needs to be filled out, or are we done?" asks Greydan.

The group while happy to see their friend doing so well continues to hold an undertone of seriousness.

"Nope, Jana took care of it all. I couldn't see it very well. She answered the questions at the desk, too … so we're good to go."

After loading everyone into JoeJoe's big black Dodge Ram Truck, JoeJoe says, "I'm hungry, can we order pizza?" Which relieves them and has them happily agreeing, and they want pizza, too.

Greydan says, "Please, call mom and dad, ASAP so they know you're alright, and so we don't get Kaden and me into trouble."

Groaning, JoeJoe takes his phone from Jana who is holding it for him and calls his mom. "Hi, mom!" JoeJoe says with excitement he isn't feeling. Jana and the others smile. Asa, having perfectly read the meaning behind JoeJoe's false emotion has to try hard to not laugh loudly.

"JoeJoe! Ricky, it's Joey! Oh, son, how are you feeling?"

"I'm fine mom, please don't worry about me. I should've ducked, but I decided to take the blow, so Greydan didn't get hit in his pretty face again." Greydan grimaces at the bad joke. Lucy Sayer doesn't think it's funny, either. JoeJoe finishes, "Mom, it isn't a big deal, really I'm fine."

"Joey, we can come home if you need. We'll come back here when things calm down at home. In fact, that's what we're doing. Ricky, get your things. Let's go home."

In the background, JoeJoe heard his father, Ricky, say, "Lucy, I can't leave. I would have too much explaining to do."

"No, mom! Honest, I'm fine. Please, don't make a big deal of it."

"Okay, son, send me a picture, so I can see your face to make sure it isn't any worse than you're letting on?"

"Sure, mom hang on." JoeJoe takes a smiling selfie that shows the small bruised cut with steri-strips. Kaden can't resist leaning into the photo with a big grin and rabbit ears behind his big friend.

"Alright, son. I guess you'll survive. But I want you kids to go right home. With that crazy out there, I don't want you guys running around. Text me when you get home, will you?"

"Yes, ma'am."

"I love you, son."

"Love you, too, mom, bye."

"Sorry, guys, I didn't want to send her over the edge with the comment about him being shot in front of you guys." Most of the time, JoeJoe uses 'guys' to mean all of them. This time he literally meant only the other guys in the group.

Kaden responds, "Not a big deal. It isn't important information and would only stir your mom up more."

The crew spends the rest of the night eating pizza and calling the other parents, then making fun of the person making the call. Each retelling went something like this,

---

"Hi mom, I'm safe."

Mom— "Did you hear about that crazy guy?"

"Yeah. That's why I said 'I'm safe. We were there, and JoeJoe got hurt."

Mom— "What? Are you okay? Is JoeJoe okay? I'll call his parents. Why were you there? You should come home."

"Yes, mom, we are all fine. JoeJoe is as fine as ever. No need to call his parents, they already know. We were getting hot chocolate. The Sayers have brought in extra security until the police say it's safe."

Mom— "Extra security ... why? Wait, do they know something? I'm calling them."

"No, mom, don't call them! They don't know any more than you do. In fact, you know more about the crazy guy than them because they're in England, and Greydan doesn't want them to come home early over this. Honest, everything is under control."

Mom—Silence. Stretching to uncomfortable silence ... "Okay, then. You stay inside the house tonight. No more running around. That wasn't very smart of you kids to be out like that. My word. In all my days, I would have never acted like this when I was your age. I love you, but ... my word. You stay inside and stay together."

"Okay, mom." The final goodbye was usually exasperated then they would all laugh about the 'overprotective parents' before the next of them called.

Jana is the last to finish, and the guys had just gotten worn out with the same conversation playing out again. As she hangs up, she glances at JoeJoe who has fallen asleep leaning on Greydan's shoulder. Greyd has his arm around his brother and is rocking him a little, singing quietly. He glances up at his girl and gives her just a little wink. This stuff warms Jana's heart for her blondie and for the love he shows JoeJoe. She is remembering the first time they had all spent the night together. JoeJoe was afraid of the thunder. Greyd had pulled him close and rocked a little. All of them saw but never shamed either of them for it. It breaks Jana's heart a little that someone who protects them so well has such need; it's one reason they're so close.

Asa crawls over to her place on the floor, sitting by Kaden's legs hanging off the couch and puts a hand on hers. She holds onto his hand and the time just stretches out into a quiet peace they all need, enjoying being together.

Greydan asks, "Kade," Greydan has only recently begun shortening his buddy's name, "he's dead asleep. Will you help me get him on the bed?"

Kaden nods and gets up being careful not to step on Jana and Asa. He holds their big friend steady while Greydan shifts, and they both take a side and lift him onto the bed. JoeJoe groans.

Kaden pats his back and says softly, "It's okay. Go back to sleep." With that, the sleeping boy settles down deeper in the covers.

When the boys join the others on the floor, Greydan says, "Jana, I'm sorry that we didn't get to rescue the prisoners today. We can try tomorrow."

"No, let's wait until JoeJoe is better. I want to be sure that going doesn't weaken him or cause a problem. I haven't seen the Creator ... I mean Eros coming forward to heal him, so it may be a few days. No matter what, it'll be all right. And if you can hear me, Eros we could really have used your help today, anytime you can come, come and help JoeJoe, too." Jana rolls her eyes as she says this last part.

Kaden pats her shoulder and says, "It is okay, sugar we'll get through this, we always do. Have you noticed how we always land on top of every situation? I think it is just how we are. If we stick together and stay positive, we'll be okay."

Jana sighs and says, "I'm glad you're that way, handsome. I need a reminder sometimes."

They all smile at her and start a movie on Greyd's laptop. Jana is snuggling into Greydan's chest halfway through the video, so they stop it for a later time and pick up their girl and lay her close to JoeJoe. The two sleeping friends snuggle together and sleep quietly while the others clean up the left-over pizza and get the other sleeping areas ready.

When they are in bed, too, Kaden asks Asa and Greydan in a whisper, "What were you guys thinking today when that asshole came into the diner?"

Greyd answers also in a low tone, "I was thinking that if I'm going to die, I want to make sure that you are all safe. When the rat hit JoeJoe, I almost rushed him but needed to hold Jana back, so he wouldn't take her. What about you, Asa? What was the guy thinking?"

"His thoughts were really messed up; all he wanted was drug money. He was very high, and he thought while he was feeling good he could get away with robbing the place. He picked JoeJoe because he thought the customers would be afraid of him. He hit him because *he* was afraid of him. At the end when the police had to shoot him, he wanted to die. Like I said his mind was a real mess. I didn't want to listen to everything. It was all horrible and dark. He had a lot of selfishness but mostly fear. Fear is something that controls a lot of people, and it just feels sick," Asa shares.

Greyd and Kaden listen and take in every word that their mind-reading friend says. He doesn't share this much at once. If they were strangers, he would never say a thing. They realize he could judge everyone because he knows what they think, but it has made him the type of guy that doesn't judge for the same reasons.

Greyd says, "Asa, if it ever gets too hard for you, just lean on me and concentrate on me and my thoughts. Maybe it'll help. I think we need to try and experiment with that some in the future. Just in case it starts to hurt you. That is something I'm sure none of us mind doing for you. In fact, the way we have the rule of holding Jana when she is in the middle of a vision and helping her with the sexual rush. I think we should do something the same for each of us. The rule with you will be to help you focus on one of us when a bad person is around in times that it might overcome you. What do you think of that?"

Asa answers, "I think I would really like that. I can ignore lots of thoughts, but the guy today was powerful like his mind was boosted."

They tell each other goodnight. Greydan is awake for a while longer, unable to sleep, thinking of what could've happened and what he could have done better. Somewhere, he relaxes and lets the worry go and drifts off to sleep.

ANOTHER DAY

A low moan wakes Jana. She rolls over to gaze at JoeJoe's pained face. His arms are tight around her, she's warm and comfortable, wishing she could stay here, wondering how he is, she asks, "JoeJoe, are you okay? I can get you a pain pill if you let me up."

Without opening his eyes, he says, "I like you right where you are and would rather have the pain than let you get up."

She giggles and responds, "Funny boy, you have to, I need to pee."

He grins, groans again, and turns over onto his back letting her go. All the boys are awake as soon as Jana goes to the bathroom. They fold blankets and put them away in Greydan's giant-sized closet. They tell JoeJoe he can stay in bed, but they're going to the kitchen to get breakfast. That's all it takes, and JoeJoe is up, making his brother's bed and rushing out the door with them.

Jana comes out of JoeJoe's bedroom in her fuzzy pj's and hands a glass of water and the meds to JoeJoe who takes them with a smile. They proceed to the kitchen where they find Chela is already making breakfast. It's waffles. Everybody loves her waffles. It's their favorite. Of course, they all like different toppings, and Chela has all the fruit and whipped cream ready for them with the flavored syrups on the counter with them.

JoeJoe is keeping up with Asa on the food consumption just fine, so the kids think he feels good enough for school. The atmosphere is happy and sunny when a newscast from the kitchen TV explains what happened yesterday. The teens had already let Chela in on the debacle when the announcer says that the criminal didn't die and is in critical but stable condition in the Duchton hospital. A shocked silence starts in the kitchen when Chela says, "I'll be right back I need to go kick his ass for hurting, mijo! She is taking off her apron and stomping away.

Greydan says, "No, Chela, please" JoeJoe is standing in front of her to block her way.

The gentle giant says, "I'm fine, Chela, and I'll miss my lunch and dinner if you're locked up because you kicked his ass."

The little cook hits his chest with a cup towel from the counter and puts her apron back on saying, "Well, we can't have you shriveling up and dying on my account, can we?"

The group of teens all laugh, agreeing when Kaden adds, "I think it's Asa that would shrivel up and die. JoeJoe might be able to last a few days!"

Now Chela says, "You might be, right what was I think-ing? Jana, I have to take care of my little ones, right?" They're all snickering then quiet as they finish eating.

The phone rings, and Kaden answers. It's his dad, and after talking for a few minutes, he hangs up. Then says, "That was my dad. He asked if I was feeling up to school. I am, so let's get ready and go.

Jana says, "Yeah, I still need to fill out my college applications with my counselor. I can't even think of having to be away from you all, and this is the first time I've had enough guts to ask, but where are you guys planning to go to college? Are we all going separately and just meeting on the holidays or weekends or are we going to go to the same school?"

"Local college is fine for me, but my parents will want a say. Dad wants me to go to NYU. I'll apply to both, but really, I just want to stay with you, too, Jana. If I get a baseball scholarship and coach says it is a for sure thing, then I can have a choice. What are the rest of you thinking?" asks Kaden.

Our parents are saying we have to go to NYU. We have the grades to be accepted, and I'm sure dad can get us in. But being away from you all will be hard for us. Can't we all go to NYU? Let's all apply there and see what happens, we all have the grades. Asa, you're the brain, so it should work. What do you all think?" Greydan asks.

Now that they see that it might be possible for them all to go to NYU, they're excited and go up to Greydan's room to get ready for class. They have a plan and will fill out the forms for college with their counselors today.

When they're ready and starting to leave the house JoeJoe says, "I just remembered that we didn't save the prisoners. Are we doing that later today?"

Jana answers, "No, we need to be sure that you're healthy first. We need to be ready for anything, so let's wait a few days. I know it's important, but there must be a reason we have to wait. What do you guys think?"

They all agree, knowing it's for the best, and they can be better prepared.

Jana adds, "We have lots to do this week anyway. The football finals are Friday, and afterward, is the Fall Formal. Then the next Friday we planned Kaden's, Asa's, and my birthday party here. I really want us all together for that dance, guys. I want to do every school thing we can so that we have great memories from this year instead of just what has been happening this past week. Did any of you get something to wear for the formal? It has to be different from what you're wearing to the prom in the spring."

"Ahhh, Jana! Noooo ...." They tease her. They already knew she would stipulate the need for different tuxes. But they tease her anyway. Jana knows them too well and isn't fooled at all. She jokingly punches JoeJoe, who is next to her, lightly on the arm. He moans like he's hurt.

"Oh, no, JoeJoe. I'm sorry!" She is leaning over to hold him as an apology, chastising herself for forgetting he is hurt.

JoeJoe grabs her and kisses her on the lips, then laughs at his own lame joke. When she figures out his little game, she pushes him away. She's laughing hard and trying to push him off but not working hard at it. After he gets up, he picks her up and carries her to his truck. The group gets in and rides together, if they need a different car, they'll just have to come back and get it.

26

HOMEROOM NEWS

*A*t school in homeroom, Mr. McCorkcle has Kaden, Jana, and Terry Ford working together on the class project when they get a new student.

Their teacher says, "Class, I want to introduce to you, Shi Luo. Please make her welcome. Shi, we have a new class project. If you work with this group, they'll catch you up. He walks her over to Jana's group. The friendly clairvoyant smiles at the new girl and asks, "Where did you get your scarf? It's beautiful."

Shi Lou breaks into a big smile and answers, "Thank you! I actually made it."

Jana introduces Kaden first. "Kaden is my boyfriend."

Shi Luo nods her head to Jana with a slight approving smirk.

"Shi Luo, this is Terry Ford."

Both of the boys greet Shi Luo before the quartet turn and begin working on their project. The kids have the whole project mapped out and just need to put it together in the last minutes of class when Mr. McCorkcle says he has another announcement to make. "Please clean up and put away your projects. I need you to consider who to vote for in the open Student Council seat for the class president."

An uneasy hush falls over the homeroom, as the students drop in their seats, anxious because Stacy Perrin was the class president. The silence is broken by the scraping of a chair on the floor.

The science teacher continues, "I know this is difficult for you. But this is part of moving on. You aren't required to forget about Stacy Perrin. But the vacant seat needs to be filled. If you don't want to elect one, the Vice-President will take the position. However, he is uncomfortable because he and Stacy were so close. All the same, you'll see sign-ups by the door on your way out. If you want to run for the position fill out the form and turn it in to me by tomorrow morning. The seniors will vote Friday. The new class president will be announced at the Fall Formal."

"Oh, I would love to do that," says Shi to the entire class and happily she reaches for the forms. *Okay, she has my vote already if she can say that out-loud when she just got here today.* Then she says, "Jana, will you and Kaden help me tomorrow? I want to pass out some flyers, so more people will know who I am and vote for me?"

"I certainly will. How about you, Kaden, do you mind? Will you give them to the baseball players and cheerleaders?"

"Sure, I don't mind. Just get me the flyers in homeroom. I'll see you later, sugar," he says.

It happens that Shi's next class is Jana's, too, so they walk together, and when they get to Mr. Janes' class, Shi walks straight up to the math teacher and introduces herself. Mr. Janes introduces her to the class, and she waves to everyone before she takes a seat in one of the front chairs. Asa grins at Jana as they settle down to study.

During the lecture, Mr. Janes calls on Asa to answer one of the more complicated formulas. Asa forgets part of one formula, so Mr. Janes asks, "Who can assist Mr. Wagner with this problem?"

Shi is first with her hand in the air waving wildly. Mr. Janes calls on her, and she finishes the formula for Asa.

For the rest of the class, Mr. Janes lets them do homework. Asa sends him a message asking if he minds if they work ahead in the book, and Mr. Janes sends him a list of the assignments until Christmas break. Asa shares it with Jana, and they get started on the next assignment.

When the bell rings, Jana and Asa are leaving the class together when Shi walks over to the duo. Jana introduces Asa to Shi as her boyfriend. Shi doesn't even blink an eye at the news that Jana has two boyfriends.

Asa is escorting Jana to her next class which she shares with Greyd. Along the way, they pass Shi in the hallway. "Shi, would you like to sit with us at lunch? I'm sure the guys would love to get to know you."

"Yes, and thank you."

"Okay, sweetie, we always sit near the stairs leading to the lobby. Just come find us there."

Shi excitedly answers, "I will!" before heading off in a completely new direction with someone else.

Jana and Asa giggle as they watch her happily bounce down the hallway.

Jana's next class is her reading class. She's already finished with her current book, so she chooses another from the eBook collection in the class syllabus. Noticing a book on Greek mythology, she checks it out and downloads it. Then she sends a message to Greyd that she has a new book titled 'The Greeks and Their (g)ods for Every Occasion,' thinking he would get a kick out of the title. He touches her and shows her his screen. Jana shakes her head as she reads the title at the top of his page. He already has the same book open and is scanning it. "I love you," she says.

At lunchtime, the cafeteria is in a buzz over the election and what it means. Surprisingly, a lot of the kids are planning to vote for Shi already. She probably wants it more than any of the others, with so little time left in the year. Jana figures Shi will get it hands down, with her being so outgoing.

Jana considers herself and the boys introverted, even though Kaden and Greyd are into sports. Kaden is probably the most outgoing, with the others taking various degrees of restraint. After Kaden, Greyd would be the most outgoing, followed by Jana, JoeJoe, and finally Asa only really talking to them most of the time. Funny thing, Asa has the warmest deep voice which will make even the most callous person take notice. He's told them that it'll come in handy for commercials. Jana is sure he's right and can hardly wait to see him on the prominent billboards and videos.

You know, maybe we should make a webpage explaining ghosts, and if someone needs help, we can help them. Jana starts to say something about it to the guys when she recognizes Shi walking toward them.

"Jana, I've been invited to sit with the cheerleaders and since I want to be a cheerleader, will you be upset if I sit with them to learn about the program here?"

"No, I won't be upset. Go sit with them and have fun. I'll see you later or in homeroom tomorrow if not before," Jana answers.

"Thank you I just didn't want to be a snob, and yeah, I'll see you in the morning," Shi says.

The new girl walks off and sits with the popular kids. Jana doesn't even notice the loss since she's already with the ones she wants to be with. She had only wanted to make the new girl feel welcome. She, apparently, does, so Jana isn't worried about her not having friends now.

Kaden answers his phone and says, "It's my dad. He's

asking if we'll come by the precinct after school." He waits to hear their answers before replying to his dad. They'll be there as soon after school as possible, but Asa may need to leave if it lasts too long.

Greydan's hand touches Jana's under the table, and he rubs her palm. She shivers. He looks at her sideways and gives her a flirty smile. She flirts back by taking his hand from under the table and lifting it to her mouth. She sucks on it for just a second then takes it out of her mouth and puts it in her lap before any of the other students at different tables notice. He tightens his legs together and breathes fast. The other boys are staring at her, frozen, wishing it had been them. Each of them are excited for the time it'll be their turn for that sexy attention. Asa looks away first, trying to adjust his pants before they have to stand up.

Kaden gets up and is about to get their trays when Jana stands up and hugs him to her and moves him back a foot in front of Asa just as a cheerleader tries to sit in Asa's lap but is now blocked. The girl decides to try again later, not knowing that the block was deliberate.

27

THE NECKLACE

*T*he crew is crammed into the good detective's office, waiting for what he wanted to tell them, when Asa holds onto Jana's shoulders with a firm grip.

Kayden's dad starts, "I would like to thank you all for helping us arrest the Perrin killer. His name is Shane Bower. Because of you, we have irrefutable proof that he is the perpetrator in this case. He has now been linked to several other killings all over the New England area. He wasn't here long. We believe Stacy was his first victim in the area, but I have information you need to know, and it is not going to be nice. Jana, had you ever seen Bower before?"

"Well, yes, sir, because he was in front of the diner quite often, and we had seen him in the park. We like to go there sometimes after dates or on weekends. That's not the only places I can remember seeing him, though. Is it important?" Jana asks.

"Only in as much that I want you to be aware he had been following you for a while. We found pictures of you in his tent and also, we found this in his pile of treasures. I know it is yours because I was with Kaden when he picked it out for you on your fifteenth birthday. I was with him and remember he stressed over finding just the right one. My son was excited when the jeweler, Mr. Martinez, came out with this one from the back." He shows her a silver necklace with a heart and five little diamonds on the face.

Jana reaches out for her necklace and turns it over the back of it is inscribed with 'my sugar.' She says, "Yes, sir, this is my necklace." She puts it on without asking if he needs it back, unwilling to be without it now. In her heart, she isn't worried so much as sick that the creep had been close enough to steal the necklace.

Jana says, "This necklace was in my jewelry box at my house in my room. I never noticed it was missing because I only take it out on special occasions. I can't imagine how he got it."

Asa still has his hands on her shoulders, helping to keep her calm. The detective says, "That was something I was going to ask. Now, what I need to know is if your parents have any cameras that might show an intruder that we can use?"

"No, sir, but I'll make sure that is on the list of things we need to do soon," Jana answers.

Then Detective Walsh adds, "Bower is set to leave the hospital this week. He's awake and getting better. He'll be sent to prison to await his trial without bail. Don't worry because the police have the criminal in hand. If all of your parents are okay with it, I think it might be best for you kids to stay under the higher security at the Sayers' home until the transfer."

Jana is the only one who even needs to ask and is sure that her parents will agree. She asks if she can call them now and dials. She really wants her parents to know she's safe, and the dirtbag isn't getting any bail. Asa's hands travel up her neck letting her know he's still here for her. She finishes her phone call then tells the detective that she'll stay with the Sayers until the creep is out of the hospital, in jail, and Mr. Walsh gives them the thumbs up that it's safe to go home.

When they get out into the front area of the police station, Greydan stops them, and they sit on a nearby bench appearing to tie their shoes and put on hats and gloves. While this is going on, Greydan is really showing them the ghost behind the desk. "He's right in front of us," whispers Greydan.

Asa says, "He's not speaking, but he's thinking that he's staying here to make sure that the evil spirits which sometimes are attached to criminals don't hurt the police who work here."

Jana looks in his direction and nonchalantly says, "That's wonderful. If you ever need any help, we're here and will do our best." She gets up and heads to the door with Asa's hand firmly in hers with the others trailing just steps behind.

When they get to JoeJoe's truck, Asa pivots and faces his girl. She reaches out and runs a finger down his beautiful face. He was there for her. He leans forward and kisses her softly, then places her hand to JoeJoe's. The meaning goes without words, they are in this together. JoeJoe nods his head then helps Jana into the front seat of his big truck. She scoots to the middle, and the other boys get in. Greydan and Kaden in the back. The way home is mostly silent except for the music playing on the truck's system. Kaden has a playlist, which he made, playing, and "Youngblood" from 5SOS is playing its upbeat tune.

When they get to the Sayers', they see that the security is even tighter than this morning. It's more like the night of Stacy's pre-wake with the football team and cheerleaders. Detective Walsh must have talked to the Sayers and made it happen. It's a good thing, too, because now Greydan won't have to do it.

With their homework finished, they go to the kitchen and snack. It's tranquil which is different. Asa walks out of the room. When he comes back, he is speaking in an exaggerated announcer voice and says, "Hello, ladies and gentlemen! Welcome to the grand opening of the very first billboard for Asa Wagoner!" He finishes the introduction with his arms spread wide and a devilish grin on his face. He hands his phone to Jana to see the picture he has open. The others stare at him in shock. Firstly, because it is Asa who came in with such an extroverted entrance, and second, because he has his first billboard.

Asa is standing there with his arms spread, the grin growing as he reads the comprehension dawning on his friends. Seemingly together, they get it and surround him. High-fives are slapped all around the room, and Chela opens bottles of carbonated apple cider.

The mood is much happier now. Any darkness left from the trip to see Kaden's dad is gone. As they retreat upstairs, Jana asks JoeJoe, "Are you okay enough to begin the mirror rescue?"

"Hell, yes! I really would like to do something that requires action."

So, this is on …

GETTING READY

*T*he crew of teens is in Greydan's big room and talking freely. They didn't say what was happening in front of any of the staff in the kitchen. Chela would box their ears; even though she knows they know about spirits, she isn't one to like them having anything to do with them.

Jana says, "Okay, this is what I'm thinking. We have our showers and get into our pj's. When we get up here, we'll sit in a circle with our books in front of us, so security will think we're doing homework. Then we can call Eros to see if he'll help. If he doesn't, then maybe he'll hear and send us an angel to either go with us or help after we get there."

As if on cue, Jana smells the flowery scent which first drew her to the mirror. She goes over to Greyd's dresser mirror and looks into it with Asa standing directly behind her. She looks into it intently before saying, "There's a spirit, Greyd. Can you see anything?"

Greydan answers, "There's a girl's spirit covered in blue light, and she's waving at us." He waves back, so she'll know he sees her. She blinks, and her eyes widen. "She's surprised at my wave."

Asa says, "That's true." To the spirit he says, "We're going to come and free you tonight. If you know anything that we need to know, I can hear you, and I'll tell the others."

He pauses and steps closer leaning toward the glass and says, "She says we can come in four hours. The one who is holding them gets drunk at nine o'clock every night. He won't be in the way. She said she'll lead us to each cell to let those who are trapped go, and there aren't any keys."

Facing the mirror, he says, "It's okay, we have someone who can open locks, anyway." Turning to the others, he says, "She said she'll give us the flower smell when it's safe. She has to go, but she says good luck and blessings over us. She hopes with all her heart this works."

The teens talk about the plan until Chela rings dinner on the intercom. they're going down in their pajamas. When Ricky and Lucy are at home, they eat at the dinner table and are expected to dress, but Chela has no problem with them eating in the kitchen in their pj's. They use the excuse that they're tired and want to go to bed early. Dinner isn't the more formal food that they usually have, but cheeseburgers and chips with fruit. The little cook tells them they have to eat some part of the meal that's healthy.

Before she leaves she asks, "Will you put your plates in the sink? I'll finish cleaning up later."

"Yes, and dinner was great," Greyd says.

Jana is excited to get started and can only eat half of her burger. Asa snags it off of her plate and finishes it. When they're cleaning up, they rinse the dishes and put them in the dishwasher, hoping to surprise Chela.

Jana notices JoeJoe is looking kind of droopy and asks, "Hey, big guy, are you okay?"

He answers pulling her into his lap, "I have a headache and need a pain pill, mí corazón. I think I'll take half a dose, so I don't get sleepy."

She puts a hand to the uninjured side of his face and says, "I think that's a good idea. Let me get it for you." She scoots off of his lap and gets his pill and a knife and neatly cuts it in half. One side shoots off hitting Kaden in the forehead. She's athletic but accident-prone. He blinks, bending to retrieve the offending mini-missile, and he says, "Are you trying to tell me something, sugar, or just trying to get my attention. Because if you only want my attention, I can assure you, it's always yours."

She sighs and ducks her head just a tad for that perfect statement then gives him a little smooch. JoeJoe pushes him playfully out of the way and says, "This is my minute, wait until I've had my pill then you can horn in."

So Chela knows they think she's special, Jana leaves her a note that they love her on the table. Then the kids head upstairs, each checking whether they sense anything wrong to be sure they're ready as individuals and a group. One and all, they're convinced that they're ready, willing, and able to proceed with the rescue.

After they position themselves strategically around the room, waiting for the signal to begin, Jana decides to try to speak with Eros one last time. So, she asks, "Eros, if you can hear me will you please come and talk to us?"

In a swirl of smoke and steam, an affectation he seems to have seized upon, he arrives with no delay. "I'm here, little oracle, how can I help? I only have a minute; my love is expecting me for dinner."

Understanding this, Jana tells him in as few words as possible what they're planning tonight. The love god puts a hand to his face and says, "I think you'll do fine. I want to send an angel with you just to be safe. It's still dangerous. He'll remain in the background and won't bother you unless you need him. Is that satisfactory?"

"Yes, it is and thank you so much." And just so he knows

she's grateful, she gives him a little peck on the cheek before he leaves with a gentle smile for 'his oracle's' sweetness.

Greydan, who's sitting closest to the mirror asks, "Hey, can you guys smell that?" Four heads turn as one toward Greydan.

JoeJoe who is on the bed, but still close, exclaims excitedly, "Yes! Wow, I haven't been able to breathe out of my nose since that ass-wipe smacked me in the head! It must be strong if I can smell it."

Jana scans his face and says, "JoeJoe turn your head to the side. Let me see your injury." His hand immediately shoots to the spot where he was hit in the head during the robbery at Maize's.

His smile matches hers, and the others look to see if they can find it. "It doesn't hurt at all anymore," JoeJoe proclaims.

"It's because it's gone," explains Kaden.

"Eros must be doing this when he visits. I wonder if he'll keep doing it when he is around, or if it's only for special situations?" wonders Asa.

"Umm, guys, the signal. We've got to get moving," Jana reminds.

The flowery smell is strong in the room now. They sit in the circle and get ready by relaxing so that Jana can pull them all into the vision/dream. She guides them into a relaxed state. "Take a deep cleansing breath in through your mouth and out your nose. Let's do it again and relax every muscle starting at your toes move up your body. Now one last deep breath and make sure your shoulders are totally relaxed. If you need to lean on each other or back on something go ahead."

This continues for a while then …

29

THE RESCUE

*T*he boys make sure they're touching one another in some fashion after Jana reminds them. "Get ready, guys. I'm going to take you into the astral plane."

Kaden and Asa who are on each side of her, shift a little bringing themselves closer. Without any fanfare, no stomach-turning tunnels or lights, their journey to the other realm is complete. Jana opens her eyes; she sees the boys are with her in the fog. It's clearing as they stand there, things are crisper and shine more brightly while the smell of flowers surrounds them. A large brilliantly lit mirror stands in front of them. It looks like a long lighted hallway on the other side of a glass pane.

A shimmer moves inside it, and Asa says, "She's here and says the clown is asleep. I don't think she's just calling that one a clown, either. I think he really is a clown."

Kaden is the first to 'walk' in this new plane. Although 'walk' is a gross exaggeration of the two small steps he takes, that's also a complete misunderstanding of what he did. His legs and feet did move, but his feet weren't touching the ground. It looks more like an avatar in a role-playing game that isn't rendering correctly, so moves oddly over objects. Or you could consider it like the words from one of the foreign films not matching the lip movement of the actors. In any fashion, it looks weird.

After Kaden float-walks to the mirror, he calmly reaches out and touches it. Kaden uses his gift to inspect the mirror. Jana watches as lights, which are on the other side of the mirror begin to move, bending it and pushing aside the energy of the surface. This creates a hole in the middle of the mirror which folds upon itself toward each edge. Finishing, he holds up a hand signaling the others to wait where they are, so he can examine the portal. The light is different now that the hole is in the outer mirror. What at first looked like layer upon layer of lights turns out to be only a single layer, reflected on a second mirror.

Kaden says, "It's an infinity mirror. JoeJoe, is it safe to touch the other mirror?"

"Sure," replies the psychometrist who float-walks over near his buddy and reaches out a big hand. JoeJoe touches the first mirror then the lights inside the hole Kaden had created. When he reaches the second mirror, he says, "This is what was holding part of Jana when she couldn't move. That magic is gone now that Kaden made the hole. The clown didn't make it, so he can't feel the change. Others made it, and he found it and uses it to trap his prisoners. That second mirror has been here for ages. The prisoners are behind it. It can't harm us now. It's alright to touch, rockstar."

Asa is the one who gave Kaden the 'rockstar' nickname. He started calling him that at their first Christmas together when his dad got Kaden a guitar that he was obsessed with and still has hanging on his bedroom wall. The baseball player has a new one that matches his size, but still loves his little first instrument.

Kaden's hands reach out lightly and causes the same

transformation in the second mirror as the first. The change is dramatic. The lighting no longer looks like a string of lights on a dingy wall. It appears very different, more like a dungeon. It's dark, damp, and has the feeling of evil and death. Those are the strongest impressions.

Asa says, "Hurry while the clown is asleep. The one who's helping us is behind this door. She's a fairy and her life is over, but her spirit is trapped here. She's warning me that if we open the door and the clown stirs, we'll be caught, too."

Kaden says, "Asa, ask her where the clown is, and I'll take care of it."

Asa answers, "She's afraid to tell and doesn't want him to capture us. I told her it'll be okay. She's stalling."

Jana leans against the door to the cell and says, "Please, we know what to do. We'll be fine."

That's when an angelic voice that they haven't previously heard says, "Little one, I'm here to take you home. I will not let these shielded ones be hurt. Come tell them, so we aren't forced to search."

Greydan says, "An angel is standing right next to Jana beside the cell door. He's beautiful and looks like a big freaking warrior. I'm absolutely sure he can do what he told the fairy."

The fairy says her name is Ana, and the clown is in the last door. Kaden goes to the last entry and without waiting for a second, opens it and says, "You will remain asleep and won't even try to wake. You will let us do our work and let us leave without trying to stop us, sleep deeper." He returns, and with his mind, he bends the lock off of the door and opens it. A small blue light of a fairy, not her body, but just her ghost is lifted by the unseen angel and taken in a blink.

Asa says, "Ana says to tell you to thank you and don't forget the others, and she said she left us a gift. I don't see anything, though."

Kaden and Jana are at the next door and perform the same thing for each cell until they reach the last one. Here Asa yells, "Stop!" With a hand on Kaden's he adds, "This cell is different. I can't hear any thoughts, no one's speaking."

All the teens move together. Greydan, who's watching the angel, says, "The angel is nodding his head. I think he's saying it is alright."

Asa says, "Yes, he is, so let's finish this."

Jana says to the door, "We're coming to set you free."

With that, Kaden manipulates the lock and the door swings open. In the bleak blackness of the empty cell is what looks like a well. Jana and the boys enter on wary feet and look down into the dark hole where there are lights on piles of bones.

Asa sucks in a breath at the number of dead and answers them saying, "Yes, we're here to rescue you." The angel gently gathers all the lights. His large loving hands holds them close before he disappears.

Greydan tells the others what he saw.

At the disappearance of their angel protector, the dungeon begins to shake as if suddenly hit by a giant earthquake. The quaking causes the jail to crumble. "Everyone out!" yells an animated Kaden.

The teens fly to the opening of the portal mirror, passing through the opening just as the prison falls in on itself. Kaden quickly touches only the second outermost mirror. Immediately it folds back out from the edges and becomes whole again. Only this time instead of the double mirror image of before they can see into the now destroyed dungeon. "I have a bad feeling," says Greydan and Jana together.

Then Asa speaks again and says, "Get us out of here, Jana, the clown is waking."

She doesn't hesitate. A moment later, they all open their

eyes in Greydan's bedroom. Each one of them has a Cheshire grin plastered on their face. The feeling of doing something for someone else that no one else could do is palpable in the room.

Jana asks her boys, "Are you all okay? Nothing out of place. Nothing missing?"

Each of them lets her know they're fine and on cloud nine. Then Greydan says, "The angel's here in the middle of our circle smiling."

Asa adds, "Yes, and he's saying that this is a noble calling. He says he's thankful to us all for caring enough to help these spirits move on to their eternal home where they can be with their loved ones. The clown was using the energy of their souls to work evil magic on the Earth for his pleasure."

Jana says, "You're welcome. It's makes us happy, too. Our passion is using our gifts to help others. If you need us in the future, we would love to assist. Or if you would like you can always help us," she adds hopefully.

Greydan tells them the angel nodded his head and left. The quintet sits quietly with 'shit-eating' grins. Just another thing completed that binds them tighter together.

Exhaustion overtaking them, they find a way to fall asleep together in Greyd's bed, having a need to be touching each other.

30

MOVING ON

*T*he next morning Jana goes to stretch awake and accidentally hits Greyd on the chest. He grabs her hand and puts it down on his morning wood. She caresses his silky hardness then wakes enough to scope the bedroom and verify that it's only the two of them. She hears someone in the shower, and hopes the water will cover any noise. Quickly, she decides to risk a quick kiss and wraps her hand back around his shaft, lightly rubbing.

He deepens their kiss as she moans, her body on fire. He puts a finger inside her hot core, and she loses the will for rational thought. The noises she makes are covered by the running water and swallowed by Greydan's kisses. His thumb planted firmly on her nerve center speeds up in response to her deepening desire. She clenches her legs together, squeezing every muscle in response to his touch. The fire pulsates its way from her, and she bucks one last time. The power of her orgasm pulls her legs wide as it rips through her.

Her muscles are jelly, her lips quiver as she asks, "Greydan, let me help you come, too." He puts her hand back on his member and pumps with her for just a little while, and he spurts his load onto her pj's grunting and relaxing into her.

His face at her neck, he kisses her and says, "I can hardly wait until we're all eighteen and can do this for real. Now, tell me why we made the pact to wait?"

That's when they hear Asa say, "Because of that kid that was eighteen and had a sixteen-year-old girlfriend that he was caught with, and the mom had him arrested. Now he's a sex offender for life. Remember we didn't want that to happen to any of us. But damn, if you two keep making me feel this way, I am going to have to get back in the shower and rub one out."

They both laugh at Asa's comment before Jana reaches for Greydan and kisses him. Then she gets up and goes to the bathroom for her shower. "I'll let you get in with me, handsome," she flirts.

"If I do we'll be late for school. But I want to, and if you promise, later I'll take you up on it. I know it won't be fair to the others since we're both eighteen. But, hun, I really want you," says Asa.

Greydan pipes up and says, "Shut up! No going back on the pact. We only have one month left. Then we can decide from there. Now get dressed, Elf twat, and let's go see what's for breakfast."

Jana smiles, twirls around, and heads to JoeJoe's shower to get ready for the day. The boys head downstairs and see that Chela made scones again. She put blueberries and raspberries in these with a little powdered sugar on top.

They're discussing their day while they eat. Asa has to go to work for a couple of hours. His boss promised not to ask often on weekdays but begged for this one time. He didn't want to say no, so he's driving his truck to school, and Kaden has baseball practice, so he'll be on his own, too. Greydan needs to stop at the doctor's so that he can be released and play in the game on Friday. So, that leaves Jana and JoeJoe to fend for themselves.

Jana sits up taller in her chair and says, "That's fine with me. I need to go home and check on my parents anyway … and get clean pj's.

After thanking Chela for the scones, they separate into different vehicles and head off for school. Jana sits beside JoeJoe in his large truck then slides out into his arms when he parks and opens the door. Sliding down his big body, she turns on again and kisses him when he bends for her. They can't get any closer as they walk into the school building. He lets her go when they get to her homeroom in Mr. McCorkle's class, where Kaden is waiting for her.

When she sits down, Shi hands her some flyers, and with a giant-sized smile, she says, "Thank you for your help, dude and dudette. I really appreciate it." Then the bell rings, and they begin working on the finishing touches of their project. Terry, who has been a little quiet, says, "I made us a working prototype of our set up if you all want to use it."

Kaden seeing the fantastic graphics says, "Are you kidding me, dude? That's amazing. We'll have an A for sure. So, you're doing that, Jana has written and printed the report and data, Shi's adding it to the poster board, and I'll give the oral report. Right?"

They all agree then Kaden adds, "I want to get it out of the way, so can we be the first to give ours? I'll volunteer, if you all agree."

With their project set, they look for any possible problems. When the bell rings for the next class, they leave with hands full of flyers that they give away on the way to the next class. Several of the students said for sure they'll vote for Shi.

Jana sits in her desk beside Asa in her math class as Mr. Janes reviews the work he wants from them. Then he lets them work at their own pace. Asa, of course, is the first one finished but Jana and a few others are soon finished. She sends a quick message to her teacher with the work file and sits back. She thinks to herself with a sly grin that she'll give her Elf Boy a treat. She imagines herself in the shower, her wet hair pulled back, her nipples erect when Asa walks into the bathroom. She pulls him to her, and hears his breath quicken beside her, so she's sure he's listening intently and ramps up her thoughts. Although he had come into the bathroom with clothes on, she quickly strips them off of him. She takes his face in her hands and says, "Asa, I love you. I belong to you. Make love to me."

A small groan behind her has her pulse speeding up as she continues with the thoughts of them in the shower together. She leans into him, and her tight nipples brush his chest, and … the bell rings. She opens her eyes and glances at her Elf Boy with all seriousness, so he knows she isn't making fun of him. He takes a breath and nods to her and says in a whisper, "I love you, too, honey."

Jana has to wait on him to regain his composure before they can leave for their next class.

When the day's done, all five of them meet in the parking lot, just like always. After agreeing on texting each other later, Greydan makes sure that everyone will still stay at his and JoeJoe's house until detective Walsh says it is safe.

31

SAFE NOW

*J*oeJoe takes Jana to her own house after school where they talk to her parents and have dinner. While they eat, the teens relay the information that they're still waiting for detective Walsh to give them the all clear that Bower is in jail before she will come home to stay. JoeJoe wants the Jays to be on guard, too.

"We had a small camera system installed. Nothing elaborate. But it'll notify us if any of the perimeters are violated again," Mr. Jay says.

Jana agrees it'll help her feel safer. She packs some more clothes for a few more days and puts her dirty clothes that she had in her backpack in her laundry basket. She'll wash on the weekend if she is home by then. Giving her parents hugs and kisses, she and JoeJoe walk to the driveway where he says, "Hold on to me, mí corazón, I don't want you to slip. It's getting slick out."

Grabbing his muscular arm and tucking her head into her jacket, she leans into her boy and says, "It's so cold it feels like full winter!"

When they get to the Sayers', they grab drinks and go to

the movie room to talk. That's where they find Greydan and Kaden talking about sports. Jana asks, "So, did the doctor release you, Greyd?"

He answers, "Yes, he did and said it's a miracle and he can't see a thing wrong with me. He had them do the X-rays twice." The teens get a chuckle from that but are glad Grey will be playing football in Friday's game.

Jana asks, "So, have you told your parents yet? When are they coming home?"

Greyd says, "Yes, I called them using my earbud while on the way home. I also texted coach. He was so happy I could hear him jumping up and down. Mom says they'll be home tomorrow. Dad finished his work and told them he can do whatever else they might need online. I also explained that the situation with Bower isn't quite over."

Asa, having just arrived from his latest photoshoot, plops down. "You know standing still for so long is a lot harder than anyone knows." The group commiserates with him before choosing to go down to the kitchen and ask Chela what is for dinner and if she wants any help.

The first one in the room is Kaden, he asks, "We came to help if you want, Chela."

Chela says, "Of course, you can help. Kaden, when does baseball season start?" Then she hands him a knife and some vegetables to pare. They are having Chinese. She hands another knife to Greydan to cut up chicken as she mixes some balsamic vinegar and honey with garlic and listens to Kaden say, "Baseball starts around February, but we're in full practice now."

She asks, "Are you still pitching?"

He says, "Yes, ma'am, I have tried other positions, but I love pitching."

The kids inform her of all they're doing, letting her know that the Sayers will be home tomorrow evening. Kaden's dad is calling. He talks to him only about a minute and with a smile hangs up then tells the crew what he said.

He says, "Dad said the weirdest thing happened. He swears that he saw a blue light over Bower early this morning when he went to check on him. All of a sudden, he had no wounds and was breathing normally. When the doctors came to check on him, they couldn't find anything wrong with him. He has a scar where he was shot, and that's all. They moved him today to a secure facility. He's in solitary confinement and won't see the light of day until his trial. Even then it'll only be a quick trip in front of a judge then back to jail." He ends with a smile.

The looks between the teens says all that needs to be said about the fairy's gift. In any event, they can't talk in front of Chela. Still, they're crazy if they think that she didn't notice. She says, "So, tell me about the blue light. I know you all know."

Jana volunteers, "Chela, we got a gift from a little blue fairy."

After a pregnant pause, the little cook says, "Fine don't tell me. I'm a big girl. I can take it."

Jana tells her, "No, really, I'm not making fun of you."

Chela blinks and says, "I've seen many things in my life, and I believe you. You be careful and don't play with Santaria, ever! It'll cause problems, and I wouldn't want to have to save your skinny asses."

They would have laughed, but the seriousness of the look on her face changes their minds, they all say, "Yes, ma'am," together.

Then the little cook puts together their dinner, and they eat until they're stuffed. After, she shoos them off, so she can clean in peace.

The kids go back to the movie room and finish their homework then pick a movie to watch. The events of the last few days have left them pretty drained, so they turn in as soon as it is over. As they walk up to Greyd's room, Jana asks, "Guys, I want to tell that blue fairy thank you, how do you guess I do that?"

Asa says, "I think you just did, and the energy around us knows and can carry it to her. No matter what, beautiful, I know she knows we're happy that she made it safe for us by healing Bower, so he can be put away."

"Yeah, I guess you're right. Just like Chela wasn't fooled for a second. I'm glad we told her the truth. I sometimes think no one notices, but I think they really do know most of the time."

Jana goes into the bathroom and puts on her pj's thinking about what happened to her others this morning and then remembers her daydream about Asa. She is almost humming with happiness when she opens the door, and all the boys are standing there listening to Asa tell them the sexiest story about what she did for him in math class. She bows her head a little when they all look her way. Then she says, "I really want to talk to you all about the pact if that's alright?"

They all agree that it's something they all have questions about. She continues, "Ever since Eros revealed that I'm his oracle, it made so much clearer to me, the way Greydan thought. He's the god of love, and if my gift comes from him, no wonder. I think my body has a mind of its own some-times, but I know if I didn't want one of you touching me, I would stop. The fact is I don't want to stop. When Greydan turns eighteen let's call game on. That's what I want. I don't want to have to think about it. I love you, and after game on, I won't be holding back. In fact, December twenty-eighth can't get here soon enough. Do any of you feel differently because I don't want to force you if you're not ready yet."

One at a time, starting with Greydan saying, "I've never wanted anything more, and I'll wait until my birthday. Hey, maybe that can be a present! No, I'm just kidding, baby, I want it to be exceptional and not forced."

Kaden says, "That's what I want, too. I want to be with you and won't be saying no, but I can wait until Greyd is eighteen, too."

JoeJoe says, I always want you and will make it special, too. Do you want us all together for the first-time, mí corazón? Can we plan this for you, or do you want to do that? It's up to you, but let me know soon? I've been hard since you turned fifteen years old."

Asa just nods, and Jana says, "Do you mind if we're all together the first time and then whenever it hits us later? Because I want to be with you all, and the first time is special."

So, in this way, a new pact is made, and this might be the longest wait ever. They all go to sleep with that on their minds but are very happy and looking forward to the life they've been ready for since they can remember.

They're all just lying in bed, awake and thinking when Jana says, "I think by the time we have our own house we'll have to have a bigger bed."

They all bust out with hoots of glee, and Greydan says, "I'm sure that we'll have a schedule by then for alone time or a way we can all be together, babe."

HOME AGAIN

*T*he weather is cold, and there are some snow flurries as the teens get to school the next morning. The halls are full of excitement. Weather tends to have that effect, but there's another reason, the race for the senior class president is heating up. Jana and the boys have been stopped numerous times as they make their way to their respective classes to be given swag and candy. Asa even got a giant cookie with a frosting ad for one of the candidates. When they sit at their desks in homeroom, they see Shi is frowning and down. Trying to make her feel better before the bell rings, Jana gives her a bright smile.

Jana says, "Hey, girlie, what's up?"

The disheartened young lady peeks at her friend and says, "I'm not sure what possessed me to run for president. I'm going to lose. No one likes me. It really is just a popularity contest, and I've only been here a few days. No one knows me."

"Well, let's think of a way we can change that, shall we?"

Jana gets out her books like Kaden had, so Shi follows them and starts to study as the bell rings. When the class breaks up into their groups near the end of class, Jana whispers to Shi that she has an idea to run past her. It takes about two minutes to get to their classes in most cases except for gym and sports. So, that leaves three minutes to do something in the hallway.

Jana says, "If you positively make a spectacle of yourself, it might garner some attention. What if you start the school fight song in the hallway when we leave here? I'll help you, and Kaden might if I ask really nicely. I wrote the words for you during class. Then next break we'll do something else that's positive and gets you more attention."

Shi says, "I love the idea. Next, I'll be with several of the cheerleaders. I might get a cheer out with one or two of them and then at lunch, too." Shi is so excited now, her frown genuinely turned upside down.

When they leave class, Jana gets all her guts up to help Shi and starts the school song as they walk. Kaden is right with them with his rich voice. He's a natural with music and is exceedingly popular, so everyone around them joins in. Shi's not only getting attention, but some students who thought she couldn't have a passion for this school have second thoughts as they join in the singing.

The trio lead a chorus of students in dancing and singing down the longest corridor of the school. It's like a high school musical come true. The scene from Footloose has even the diminutive, introverted Jana singing, dancing and smiling all the way to her next class. Before she's able to duck inside the door, she feels a tug on her arm and is completely swallowed with a hug from Shi. It only lasts a second then she's moving on, still singing with other students.

The bell rings, and Jana sits in her seat next to Asa. He's beaming, his model-perfect teeth on full display when Jana says, "Well, my work here is done!" They both chuckle.

Mr. Janes, looking sternly over the top of his wire-rimmed glasses, tells them, "If you two would like to keep talking, you're welcome to come to the front and share with everyone." Deciding they didn't want that option, the two settle down fast.

At lunch when the crew meets at their table for lunch, JoeJoe's healthy voracious appetite has returned. He has a tray, piled with food that they all start on. Of course, Asa has his own outsized plate all to himself.

Jana glances over when she feels the excitement around her and watches as Shi, and several cheerleaders do a routine in the middle of the room using the V-I-C-T-O-R-Y chant as a template.

> "S-H-I-L-O-U-Why?
> Shi Lou's got school spirit, that's right!
> S-H-I-L-O-U-Why?
> She'll fight for us without a rest!
> S-H-I-L-O-U-Why?
> Shi Lou's clearly above the rest."
> After the cheer is finished, she asks for
>   everyone's vote on Friday.

"That was amazing," exclaims Jana. "And everyone is buzzing about the fight song and the cheer!"

"It looks good for her now. The kids here are deciding that we need new blood for the best ideas," says Asa. Jana nods her head with a wink.

Then leaning over to JoeJoe, she says, "Lean over the tray just a sec."

He does so without question, and good thing, because someone threw a mostly empty milk carton. It hits JoeJoe in the back, bottom down, before careening off and onto the floor. It would have landed in the middle of their food. Instead, it's a slight mess at their feet. The guilty kid now has extra-large eyes and apologizes as he cleans up his mess. The offender has his back to them and doesn't speak again as he hurries to get away from their table.

JoeJoe, true to his nature, forgives the kid and returns his attention to their table, ignoring the kid's fears.

Greydan asks, "My parents will be landing about an hour after the last bell. Who wants to go with JoeJoe and me to the airport? We can pick them up now that it's safe."

Kaden says, "I can't. I have practice until five. Then dad wants us to have a family dinner."

Asa says, "I can't, either, there's a shoot tonight. It'll take several hours. I might not be home until dark. Make sure and text me, though, so I know they are safe and sound, okay?"

"I'll go with you," Jana says slipping her hand in his.

The kids clean up their trays and get ready for the rest of their day. Shi catches Jana on the way out and says, "Thank you, you're a genius. I won't forget you helped me."

After the last bell rings and they are released, Greydan, JoeJoe, and Jana tell the others goodbye in the school parking lot to head to the airport and pick up the Sayers. They stop and get drinks for the trip at the corner convenience store then continue on their way. They are teasing each other as they wait in the air terminal and don't even notice Ricky and Lucy standing in front of them until they say, "Hey, kids!"

With big mom hugs, Lucy excitedly tells Jana about all the girl stuff. The boys roll their eyes to raze them as they get in the car for the ride home.

Greydan says, "Bower, is tucked away in prison. We shouldn't have to worry about him anymore. I'll drop Jana off at her house before we go home if that okay?"

Ricky replies, "Hang on a second, son, let me call and make sure." Mr. Sayer calls Detective Walsh and is assured that everyone is safe from the killer, and he is definitely put away.

Greydan pulls up to Jana's home and gets out to tell her goodbye. He hugs her, standing in front of his brother who shields them from their parents' view. He just brushes his girl's lips with a quick kiss then lets JoeJoe do the same. He's also fast and guards her with his body and brings his shoulders up, kissing her with just a touch and go smack. When they get back in the vehicle to leave, neither looks at their parents as they drive away.

33

THE WINNER IS

A few days have passed, and it's already Friday. Almost every student is excited and busy. There's so much going on that it's hard to concentrate on their studies, and their teachers know it. The school is filled with the kind of teachers who want them to enjoy learning and who know that school spirit is part of the process. Because of this, most of them have assigned a lighter set of assignments than usual for today. In fact, some of the teachers seem to be almost as excited to participate, as the band, cheerleaders, and football players storm the halls. Storming the halls is a tradition where the school band plays upbeat tunes in the hallways moving at a fast pace. The cheerleaders and football players run and dance. It garners excitement for the ballgame that evening, and students are encouraged to join in.

Jana is so proud of Greydan in his football jersey, and only has eyes for him. She's watching for him when she's bumped from behind by a guy in glasses who smiles and asks her, "Do you want a piece of this?" He is pointing to himself.

She vigorously shakes her head side to side and says, "No." But the noise in the hall is pretty loud, so he may not have heard her. Still, he had to see the head shake. Nevertheless, he reaches for her, and with a hand around her waist, begins pulling her to him. Jana struggles to escape his grasp when, like Adonis riding on Pegasus, Asa arrives and pushes the guy away.

Asa just looks skinny. Under his clothes, he's solid muscle and power. Loudly enough so that the punk has no problem hearing, Asa tells him, "She said no. No means no, punk. Leave her alone!" The shit-head puts up two hands in front of him in the universal 'I don't want a beef with you' gesture and backs away, red-faced.

Jana swallows hard, trying to regain her composure and hugs Asa, putting her face to his neck. Her whole body is shaking. He whispers into her ear, "I'm here. Everything is all right now, honey. I won't leave you alone until one of the others is with you, okay?"

She nods approvingly holding his shirt when she hears the announcement, "All students report to the auditorium to vote for your choice of class president."

As they walk, Jana relaxes some as the music and excitement of the band and players rubs off on her again, but she keeps her head down. They enter the auditorium and walk around to several kiosks with flaps on the side for privacy, and vote. It happens that there are only three candidates. The kids make their choice and move to sit in one of the chairs. Jana waves at Shi who is seated on the stage several yards in front of the clairvoyant. All of the boys find her and Asa, and sit together with them on the padded chairs set in rows.

Pretty soon their principal Mrs. Scott is making announcements and giving instructions on how to get tickets for the football game and the fall formal afterward. Greydan holds up all of the group's tickets with a wicked grin. As one of the starters and one of the best football players, he gets his tickets for the game from his coach. He just has to tell him how many he wants and receives them. Jana grins at him and is quietly glad he always takes care of their tickets. She's not sure that Asa's family would have been able to afford them when they were in grade school. JoeJoe certainly wouldn't have been able to if he hadn't been adopted.

Mrs. Scott takes an envelope from her vice-principal Harry Owens and makes a big deal of ripping it open, then announces … "And the winner and our new senior class president is … Shi Luo!"

Everyone claps, and Shi moves to the podium and gives a short nervous speech unable to wipe the smile from her tiny face. Mrs. Scott takes the mic back and gives a few rules for the formal and that no drinking or fights will be tolerated. She says, "Security will haul you off to the police station in cases where alcohol is found. So, students show up with your dancing shoes on, and we'll have a great time tonight. We're dismissing early today. See you tonight. You may leave."

The teens leave, and for a change, they each go to their own homes and aren't together directly after school. Jana says, "I'll meet you guys at the football game."

Shocked faces stare back at her as the four guys react to her surprising announcement. Asa is the first to speak, "Are you sure? I don't like you being alone after what happened when we stormed the halls."

JoeJoe quickly chimes in, "Wait a minute what happened?" All eyes are on Jana, expecting her to answer.

Jana explains what happened, then adds, "I'll be fine, guys, honest. I'm going to do girl stuff. You know … a mani-pedi, hair … there will be tons of people around. Although, if you want to go, I think I'd love it. In fact, let's all do it together!" She giggles at the faces they're making, then adds, "Mom will be with me, so really, don't worry. I'll let one of you pick me up, how is that? You decide between you and the rest of you smexy boys … I'll see you at the game."

34

FALL FORMAL

*W*hen Jana and Nichole get home from the spa, they're both happy and excited to be dolled up. Nichole shows Jerry her new hair and nails, and he whistles as he walks around her, bobbing his head appreciatively before giving her a hug with a growl. He watches his little girl then scoots back some and says, "Turn around, honey so I can get the full vision."

Jana spins in a circle for her dad. She can't wipe the smile from her face and then the grin drops when she notices he isn't happy and asks, "You don't like my hair, dad?" Her long locks are curled and shiny down her back.

He answers, "I love it! You're gorgeous, sweetheart. I don't think I should let you in public looking so beautiful and grown up." He puts an arm around Nichole and sniffs. "Honey, our baby has grown up on us."

Nichole pops him on the chest lightly and says, "You dog, I thought you were serious at first. Yes, she did." She brings her gaze to her daughter with a proud stare and adds, "You *are* gorgeous, honey. Do you need money for tonight?"

"I have plenty and probably won't need it tonight,

anyway, mom. Thank you." She goes up to her room to get into her outfit upstairs and is putting on a jacket when the doorbell rings. It's one of the guys and a surprise since she let them decide who would pick her up.

When she comes down the stairs, Kaden's standing in the foyer with a huge football corsage, complete with ribbons hanging to the floor. He looks so cute, and a bit shy. Looking up, his Adam's apple bobs with a gulp. Jana scans the beautiful status symbol closely, it has all the boy's names on one of the ribbons, but Greydan's is in the middle written in a slightly larger font. Her handsome boy just stands there frozen until Nichole helps, "Kaden, let me help you pin this on."

They pin it on, and it's as long as the wearer. Jana is beaming as her shoulders raise, and her smile widens even more. The corsage is a rite of passage for the football game before the fall formal, and the ones who get one from a love interest are set on the pedestal of teen admiration.

Jerry takes tons of pictures. Kaden is so good at this that the poses are second nature to him. After posing for one last photo, Kaden 'helps' the two senior Jays understand it's time to go using his gift of manipulation. After he hands his girl into his car, he tucks all the ribbons in and leans in for a kiss. His touch is soft until his girl opens her lips encouraging him to deepen the kiss. When he understands she wants him just as much as he wants her, he pulls her to him and gives her the kiss he wants. They continue for just a little bit before he pulls back and says, "We need to leave for the football game, or we'll never make it."

On the way he says, "Jana, I think you're beautiful no matter what, but tonight, I think you look amazing. Thank you for doing that for us."

She says, "Well, right now, this is just for you. You make me wish I was even more than what you think I am because

I think you are so hot that I'm the luckiest girl in the world."

His shoulders square in his seat, and he sits visibly taller. When they park, he gets another kiss and lets his date out. They walk hand in hand to the gates, turn in their tickets, and enter the stadium. She finds Asa and JoeJoe, and she runs, pulling Kaden to them. The boys all stand when they see Jana and hoot how pretty they think she is. JoeJoe sits and pulls her onto his lap, telling the others he'll share later, right now this beauty is his. The national anthem starts, and everyone stands, JoeJoe has Jana stand in front of him. The pressure of her back against him is intense but well worth the tension. They stay standing and watch as the football players take the field. Cheers and whistles are loud in their ears, and they add to the den when they see Greyd.

When it's all said and over, the Erie High Golden Knights win the game hands down. It was close at the end of the first half, but the Knights took complete control in the second half, making it's a blowout. As usual, Greydan makes some fantastic plays. The teens quiet when they hear a scout behind them point out their buddy and name Greyd by name. They'll tell him about that for sure. Ricky and Lucy were up a few seats and surely, heard the comments, too.

The plan now that the game is over is to wait for Greyd then go to the Sayers and get dressed for the dance. Jana's dress is there, and Lucy has already promised the Jays lots of pictures. The Jays are out on the town, anyway. Greydan comes out into the cold air with his hair still wet, and Jana rushes him, praising his athleticism. He swings her around and lets her go when his mom hands him his coat and says, "Hurry, it's cold out here. We have to get you all dressed for the dance. The limo will be ready in an hour."

Lucy helps Jana into her dress and adds the girlie primps to her hair and then says, "Jana, you look beautiful!" As Lucy pulls her in for a hug, tears form in Jana's eyes. Lucy gently taps at them so as not to smear Jana's perfect makeup. "Are you ready to go down now, young lady?"

"Yes, ma'am."

"Okay, dear, I'll go first, take a minute then follow me downstairs." Lucy flies down and tells the boys she's coming down and to stand up and wait for her, so she'll feel extra special. She also grabs a camera, and Ricky Sayers grabs his phone. The first thing Jana sees as she descends the stairwell is the quartet of boys standing at the foot of the stairs, a look of awe on each face. They are each wearing tuxes with something matching her plum and silver formal, from pocket hankies to the color of their vests and shirts. Her heart swells with love.

Greyd saunters over to her and helps her with the last few stairs in the heels that Lucy calls 'two-hour shoes.' Asa has the door open, and JoeJoe has the limo door open now. Greyd releases her to get into the car, and Kaden makes sure to tuck the length of her dress into the car. After everyone is seated, the limo slowly pulls away and heads toward the dance.

It is quiet in the limo then, all at once, all the boys burst out at once to tell Jana how beautiful they think she is tonight. When they get to the front doors of the dance, Kaden holds her hand to help her out, and Greydan meets her to guide her into the hall with JoeJoe on her other side. Asa is holding the door this time, and Kaden makes sure her dress doesn't get stuck in the door when it closes.

The dance is a fairy tale of twinkling lights and atmosphere. Several of the girls come to tell Jana how much they love her dress. Shi is there and gives her a hug in her own fantasy dress. Jana says, "Congratulations on your win, Ms. President. I hope it's everything you want it to be."

Shi says, "Why thank you, Jana, one of my esteemed

cabinet members. I'm so happy! I think that the committee and I will be able to do some nice things for our class this year. You should join."

Aw thanks, that is nice, but I try to stay far away from school politics," Jana answers.

Greydan asks, "May I have this dance, Jana?"

His girl smiles and says, "Why yes, you may." Jana smiles at Shi, and the girl nods to her, letting her go dance with her handsome boyfriend.

The music is busy, and thumps then changes to a slow song, and Greyd pulls Jana close. They're touching from her face on his chest to their knees, swaying to the tunes. Greydan kisses her on the top of her head then whispers in her ear, "I feel guilty that I'm the reason we all have to wait for 'game on.' Jana, if the pull gets to be too hard you can always have your first time with one of the others. I promise I'll wish it is me, but I won't be upset. I think we have talked about this enough over the years that you know how we feel. I just want you to know my part about having to wait."

Jana lifts her gaze to his and says, "It's not going to hurt me or the others. Don't feel guilty. It's something we want for all of us, and the wait is worth it. How will you all really feel about it when it gets here, and we are all legal, though? Is it crazy to be all of us? Will you be comfortable?"

Greyd responds, "I have no problems with that. It has been an impossible dream of mine for a while. I'll be glad and privileged. Then when we can and are together alone, I'm going to die of happiness!"

Jana says, "Nope, no dying." She titters then sighs, "That's how I feel, too. We can do this, but it is hard to wait."

Asa moves up as the song finishes and asks Jana for the next dance. Greydan walks off the floor to talk to some of the football players about the game. The night is a dream for them all, and they dance and change partners then dance some more. Jana is ready to sit a few out when she finishes dancing with JoeJoe. They sit at one of the decorated tables and have some finger food and a drink.

Jana takes a big drink of her drink and says, "I was thirstier than I thought.

JoeJoe starts to jump up for more, but Jana puts her hand on his and says, "I have enough, mí corazón." She calls him the same name he calls her, they have for a long time. He smiles when she does it, so she'll never stop. The others join them at the table with some cake and bring Jana some, too. She takes it and eats some, thanking them.

The dance is almost over, and it's getting late, so she asks if they're ready to leave. "I would like to ride around some in the limo before we go home." That's what they do before they take her home where each boy gets out and walks with her to the door. They all crowd around her, touching, and give her a little kiss then let her go inside. They all high five each other, then the driver takes them all home to dream happy dreams.

35

THE REPORT

*T*he formal was perfect, and Jana lives in the euphoria for the entire weekend. Then it's over before she even had time to notice it was here. Her boys were so perfect and made her feel so special that her feet only touched the ground earlier this morning. Well, it's time to get ready for school; the report is due, and her team does want to go first.

Lots of students in the hallway are still as high as she was from the weekend and are extra noisy today. Calming down to study with the holidays coming is going to be a challenge.

Shi stops by her locker and says, "I know you had a good time Friday night, but damn, girl, you can wipe the smile off now. On second thought, just remembering you dancing with your horde of sex on a stick put it back on."

Jana responds, "I know, huh? I'm a lucky girl, you can congratulate me all you want. They are hot."

They are giggling as Kaden saunters up to walk Jana to class. Shi gives her friend a conspiratorial wink and walks ahead of them to class. They go into the room, sit, and gather the stuff for the report when Terry sits down with them. Mr.

McCorckle calls roll and makes all the announcements for the assignment and starts, "You have all had plenty of time to finish your team reports. Who would like to do their report first?"

Kaden's hand shoots up, and he doesn't wait for an answer and stands. He drags Terry to the front, asking him to set up the poster with the graphics up in front. Their teacher is lagging with his acceptance and mockingly says, "Why yes, Mr. Walsh and Mr. Ford, go right on and let us have the pleasure of the information you and your team have collected. Impress me."

Terry sets up the tri-fold poster and hands a pointer to Kaden, which he takes with aplomb and flourishes it for affect. The students laugh at his antics and settle in to listen as he gives the report. He is a performer, and his deep melodic voice keeps them interested in natural energy, for the few minutes it takes to get through the information. When he's finished, their instructor claps, and the class follows his example. The next volunteer steps up to the front of the room to take their team's turn.

When Kaden sits next to Jana she notes he is sweating and cocks her head and brow at him. He whispers, "It's harder than it looks. I was faking ease, but it's a rush. It's sort of like throwing the first pitch of a state championship game."

"Holy crap, Kaden. I can't even imagine. I almost get sick with just the thought of speaking in front of everyone," Jana whispers back.

They had time for several other reports, but about half the class will have to share theirs tomorrow. When the bell rings, many of the students pat Kaden on the back as they walk out the door. He smiles and says, "It was nothing, Jana, Shi, and Terry did the hard work."

Jana slides under his raised arm and gives him a quick

hug before moving onto her next class. She pats his butt and lets go saying, "See you at lunch, rockstar."

❧

THE CREW MEETS in the cafeteria as usual for lunch. They are instantly worried at scanning the room to find JoeJoe isn't there. He's like clockwork with the big tray they are used to seeing. In fact, they can't find him at all. The rest of them meet where he should be at their table. Jana's breath is hurried, her brows are knit, and hands wringing when she almost sobs, "Asa?"

Asa answers, "I hear him. Follow me, he's close."

Greyd pulls out his phone at the same time as Kayden. The dark-headed boy nods to his blond friend to take the honors and text his brother. When the group gets around the corner, in a space that the students use for a waiting area before the principal's office, they spy the big guy and hold back. Greydan goes forward with Kaden to help but also stops and watches the big guy handing a burrito to the secretary. Kaden motions for the group to hurry back to the cafeteria by swooshing his hands forward and back a few times. They take off. When they get back to the lunchroom Asa says, "Grab us a tray with enough for JoeJoe will you, Greyd? We're going to sit at the table like nothing and wait. I'll tell you what happened when you get there."

The tall blond football player just makes it to a seat at the table with the food when his brother comes in and sits with them. Asa doesn't get the chance to say anything and lets JoeJoe tell his own story.

Squeezing into the chair next to Jana, JoeJoe stares at Greydan and says, "Sorry I'm late. And thank you for getting our lunch today, bro. I saw Mrs. Collins, the secretary, dropped her food and just left embarrassed without getting anything. I picked it up for the janitor and knew she didn't have enough change to get anything else, so I took her a burrito from the snack bar."

Greydan pats his brother on the back and Kaden says, "That's how we do it. Did she give you a couple of free hall passes for your thoughtfulness?"

Jana shakes her head and guffaws louder than the boys. When they stop laughing, she asks, "Guys, is it alright if we let Lucy do our birthday and not dress up? I'm kinda wanting to just veg and rest up for a while."

Kaden and Asa both agree since it will be their party, too, and they are all a bit happy not to have to dress up. Now to get ready for the holidays and party so close together. No black Friday for them!

36

OUR HOLIDAY

*T*he formal was perfect, and Jana lives in the euphoria for a time. The holidays are here, and they have a few days off of school for the Thanksgiving holiday. It has been several days since the dance, and the crew are about to celebrate Thanksgiving dinner together.

They have a full day of eating with different parents. Jana's parents like to cook at noon, so they start there then go to Kaden's then to Greydan's in the evening. Asa loves it and is always ready to eat more. This is his favorite holiday. They really only eat dessert at Kaden's' house, and the family is used to that, knowing that they have already eaten and will be eating more later, now that the teens are older, and all their parents are used to them wanting to be with each other. Kaden's mom is the only mom who ever tried to break them apart, and she only did that one year. Kaden was so depressed that she changed her mind about the 'only family' rule and let him have his friends with him. Then as they got older, she eased up on letting him leave and go to the other parents also. The Sayers always invite the other parents, but none of them go because of their own celebrations, but this year Jana's parents decided to go because they want to be with the kids as much as they can before they move and don't see them as much.

They're just leaving Kaden's house with Kaden following behind and are headed to Greydan and JoeJoe's when Asa asks, "Do you mind stopping at my house for a bit?" He'd managed to drop some cranberries on his shirt, and the Sayers party is more formal, so he really does need to change.

They are in JoeJoes's big truck, so they stop and let him off, so he can change and come in his own vehicle. They plan for Asa to bring Jana home after the dinner party.

Jana scoots out with her Elf Boy and says, "I'll ride with Asa and see you there in a few minutes. Okay, guys?"

She gets out and goes inside with Asa as the brothers drive away. Asa is unlocking the door to his house when he says, "I wish my parents were home and could go with us."

Jana feels bad for him and says, "It must be hard to always be alone, handsome. If you want to stay with me all the time, you can."

He says, "I'm alright, honey. Jana if you want me to, I will move in with you when your parents move. I'm sure that the others will be happy you are not alone, too. I know I will be."

"I think that's a great idea. Let's plan for it and make sure the others know just in case they have been worried, okay? Anyway, Happy eighteenth birthday, Asa. I have a present for you for tomorrow at our big party, but I just want to tell you today."

They go up to Asa's room, and Jana waits outside his door, so he can change. He motions her in and says, "Nothing you have not seen or won't soon anyway, hun." He makes a little dance for her and whips the stained shirt off then reaches for her and asks, "Can I have a kiss and touch you just for a minute before we leave?" That is when they hear the sound of talking and people coming into the house. They both leave Asa's room and see that his parents are home. He smiles and walks to them with hugs, Jana right behind him.

Darren Wagoner, Asa's dad, says, "What is going on here, son?"

His mother, Kerri Wagoner, is frowning and says, "Yes, Asa, please tell us. We came home to surprise you for the holiday and find you half dressed with a girl in our home. What were you doing with her upstairs?"

Asa and Jana are surprised by their actions and back away from them as Asa says, "This is my girlfriend Jana, and you have met her before. I was changing my shirt because I messed it up. Nothing happened, and we are on our way out."

His dad isn't happy with his answer and says, "It is obvious that more was going on, I'm just glad we managed to come home before it went any further. I'm sorry, young lady, but you need to leave. Asa, you go get some clothes on, now!"

Mrs. Wagoner's mouth is set in a grim line and agrees. She opens the front door for Jana to leave.

Asa says, "I'll be right there."

The next thing Jana knows, she's standing on the porch alone as the door shuts in her face. Feeling that she did something terrible and thinking she might need to apologize, she stands there for a minute, then on second thought, decides to walk home and get her car then go to the Sayers and tell the others what happened.

She is a block away when she notices Asa in his truck pull over and stop. She gets into his side as he gets out to let her in.

She apologizes, "I'm so sorry, handsome. I didn't mean to cause trouble. Do you think that you should go stay with them or at least invite them to the Sayers tonight?"

"No, not after the way they just treated you. It got worse after you left, and dad ordered me to my room. I went and changed then packed a bag then when I started out the door he told me I wasn't leaving. I told him I am leaving we have a dinner to go to. He pushed me and said I was staying, so I pushed him back and told him that I'm eighteen, and I'm leaving. I don't even think they know it is my birthday today."

"Asa, I'm so sorry. You can stay with me for sure. I wonder what happened that made them so angry."

"I don't know, but taking it out on you is wrong, and I won't let that happen."

They are calming down as they pull up to the Sayers and push the gate combo to get into the drive where they're met by the happy faces of Greyd and JoeJoe's parents. They give Jana a hug, and Ricky shakes Asa's hand, but Lucy is not having it and hugs Asa tight and tells them both Happy Thanksgiving and remembers to tell Asa, "Happy birthday." Then says, "The others are in the party room. Now you are going to be here, tomorrow, right? I planned the birthday party for you all. Greydan will have to wait, but the rest of you will get to celebrate tomorrow."

Jana answers, "We wouldn't miss it, Lucy," Then as Jana passes Lucy she whispers, "And thank you for remembering that it is Asa's birthday."

The music is on in Greyd's room as they enter. JoeJoe and Greydan are already dressed as are the new arrivals. They're just waiting on Kaden now. They don't have to wait very long before their fifth is walking in the door with a big smile.

Kaden winks first at Jana then says, "Did I tell you happy birthday yet, Asa? If I didn't, then happy birthday, Elf Boy." Kaden teases with Jana's nickname for their friend.

"Yes, you did at your house," replies Asa without adding what had just happened at his own.

Jana lowers the boom and says, "Asa's going to stay with me for a while. He might as well, he's there most of the time, anyway." She doesn't tell what happened, either ... that's his story to tell.

Greydan says, "I know you can take care of yourself babe, but I feel a lot better knowing that you won't be alone when your parents move, and I think they will be happy about it, too."

That's when Lucy Sayer shows up at the door and says, "Kids, the staff is setting the table. Will you come down to eat, please?"

They all say they will and trail after her like baby ducks. When they get to the dining room, the room is a sight to behold, and the smells of the Thanksgiving dinner are lovely.

Asa's stomach growls, and JoeJoe laughs then says, "I'm so glad I'm not the only one that is beyond ready to eat again."

Everyone laughs knowing how much Asa and JoeJoe can put away at a meal. JoeJoe is standing close to Jana, so he seats her like a gentleman, and Greydan seats their mom. When they're all seated and have their plates full, Ricky Sayer says a prayer of thanks, after which, everyone digs into the feast.

This is no time for quiet, and everyone is sharing and talking. They have a lot to be thankful for and take turns with the stories. The whole room has a positive vibe, and the dinner is great. When they finish, the teens all go into the kitchen to tell them thank you and give Chela a hug for the wonderful meal. Then they all go to the movie room and watch football as a group.

Before it gets dark, everyone is leaving, giving hugs and kisses and thanking the Sayers. Lucy says, "You are all welcome, and I will see you all tomorrow for the party. We are planning a fun day, so don't be late."

All the teens tell each other goodbye, promising each other they'll text later to say goodnight then leave for the night.

37

THE BIRTHDAY PARTY

*E*ven though the day is sunny and bright the next morning, it's cold. It's warm in the Jay's kitchen, though. Nichole is making breakfast. Asa is a little down, and she takes note of his visage and asks, "Asa, honey, do you need to talk about something? I can tell something is wrong. You can always talk to me if you need to."

Jana is shocked when her boy opens up to Nichole, but really if she thinks about it, her mom has been there for him more than his own parents.

Asa says, "Nichole, I feel horrible about having to stay here. My parents are actually home."

The older woman smiles, not understanding.

Asa continues, "We had a big fight because I was changing my shirt and Jana was with me. I had gotten it dirty, and we were on our way to the Sayer's house for Thanksgiving dinner, so we stopped, so I could grab a fresh one. I had just taken off the dirty one when my folks got home."

Nichole understanding now, nods and listens for to him finish.

He adds, "They both thought the worst of us and told Jana

to leave. They rudely put her out on the porch and closed the door in her face. You, and everyone but them, wished me a happy birthday yesterday, they didn't even remember I turned eighteen. I left after pushing my dad, and I can't quit thinking about it. Today, Lucy is making Jana, Kaden, and I a great big birthday party, and I don't want to be a downer, but I feel awful."

That was the most words they'd ever heard Asa speak at once, so they understand how much this bothers him.

Nichole says, "Hun, most of the time there's something else wrong with the person who is mad. Sometimes, it doesn't have anything to do with their target. Even if it were you that they were upset with, maybe they're calmer now and ready to listen. Would you like to call them and talk? We'll give you privacy if you want. If that doesn't work, do your best to get over it and not let it control you."

"I think I will try to call them. I don't have to be alone. If you don't mind, I'll call now," he says.

"Of course, we'll be here for you if you need us," Nichole answers. Jerry is just coming in and sits to start eating when Asa stands and calls his parents. But the yelling they hear over the phone starts before Asa even says a word.

The quiet boy takes over and says, "I want you to know that yesterday was my birthday, and you're the only people who didn't remember that fact. You accused me of something that didn't happen without any facts and basically threw my girlfriend out of the house into the cold. She was walking home when I got to her. I don't understand why when you have known her most of her life. If you really didn't want me in your life, you just needed to tell me." A short pause then, "No I won't be coming home. I'm of legal age to decide, and I don't see a reason to, but you do have my number if you want to call later."

Asa looks up at the Jays with a distressed look and says,

"Okay, it's a little better now," he says, putting a forced smile on his face.

Jerry Jay pats him on the back and says, "Now that's a great way to be, Asa, proud of you." After Jerry finishes eating, he informs Jana and Asa that they're going out and will see them later. The teens get ready for the party and leave.

When they arrive at the Sayer's home and are getting out of Asa's truck, Kaden, JoeJoe, and Greydan step out of the front door with Ricky and Lucy close on their heels. The Sayers rush them into JoeJoe's big truck with the only instructions being, "Follow us."

While following the Sayers, they discuss their destination. Not one of them has a clue. Left with only one option, the crew just does what they're told and follows the Sayers.

Soon, they arrive at a giant warehouse with a big sign which reads, 'The Best Escape Rooms Anywhere!' The excitement in the big black Dodge is palpable now. Excitedly, they jump out of the truck and wait in front of the building while the Sayers talk to the manager. Jana can't hear what's being said, but she does hear the manager laugh as she points to an area where a guide is waiting for them.

The guide has some rules and tips to go over with them before they enter. The teens are so excited that they can hardly stand and are shifting from foot to foot but still listening, so they don't miss anything that might help them win the challenge. They have a large group, but the team they are going up against is nowhere to be found.

"Where do you think the other team is?" asks Jana.

"Something isn't right with this," responds Asa. "I know my ..."

Suddenly, an even larger group than theirs begins to move in their direction. "What in the world is going on?" wonders Asa and Kaden together.

The group moves out of the darkness and into the light, and the crew of teens recognizes their parents ... all of them ... even Asa's.

He immediately walks over to them and says, "That was great! You fooled me."

His dad, Darren says, "Sorry, son, but it was the only way we could think of to surprise you. We didn't mean to be cruel. Do you forgive us?"

"Well ... yes, I do," says Asa who laughs and says he really did believe that they forgot his birthday.

His mom gives him a big hug and says, "Never, my beautiful boy. We came from halfway across the world just to be at your party. Jana, we're sorry we did that to you, too."

Jana is crying tears of joy at seeing her Elf Boy 'reunite' with his parents. She hugs both of Asa's parents before responding, "I understand now. He is tough to fool!"

The reunion finished, Mrs. Wagoner says, "Now, let's see if you young guns can even get through this room. We're about to beat the pants off you." She is laughing as she hugs her son then Jana again.

Asa says, "Come on, guys we have to win." Then to the parents he points and says, "It's so on!"

The guide takes the teens into another room and explains, "If you can't figure out how to escape, you can have clues. But when you ask for clues, it will bring down your score." So now, they're even more determined to win without clues. The door closes, and they are left to figure out how to get out. JoeJoe is so tall the first thing he notices is a note hanging off of a mirror, which of course brings back the memory of the other realm. He quickly grabs it and reads it. It says, 'Little things are reflected in others.' So, they look in the mirror and find hanging behind them is a string which hangs down over a table Asa crawls under the table, they all go to him and he says, "So, you guys want me to tell you where we're going, or do we play this clean?"

They all laugh and decide to play with their gifts and surprise their parents. The parents are the ones who started with the fooling thing. So, let's do this! Asa says the door is behind that big box that looks like a bookcase. They all walk over to it and swivel it open and walk out.

The guide is so surprised that he stammers but collects himself and has the parents follow him. The fantastic thing is that the parents are out almost as fast as the teens. Which makes them redouble their efforts. By the end of the next three rooms, the manager and the guide are cheering them on, profoundly invested in the game.

In the end, the teens win. But only because the parents asked for a clue in the last room. It was just enough. When everyone walks out, huge smiles adorn every face.

There is a mini-caravan of vehicles returning to the Sayer's for cake. Yes, they had cake, and a couple dressed in extravagant costumes called the Kissing Cowboy, and the Kissing Cowgirl tease the teens with kisses and songs. Greydan makes the mistake of saying, "I'm glad my birthday is next month. I want a small party."

Hearing that, the Kissing Cowgirl sits in his lap and smooches all over his face before she gets up. Chela wheels out a cake taller than her, and the parents and Greydan sing "Happy Birthday" to the others then watch as they open presents.

They got some lovely presents for their milestone birthdays. Jana got her grandmother's diamond ring, a gift certificate to her favorite clothing store, and a bank account that her parents had started when she was a baby. Asa got a new truck and funds for college. Kaden got funds for college and his gramp's truck. Detective Walsh and his wife were in a hurry to get home, so they left first then the Wagoners, who told Asa it was alright if he didn't come home, but they'll welcome him back correctly when he does. Then Jana's parents said their goodbyes and left last.

As the teens are helping clean up, they start dancing with Chela. They spend a long time playing songs and dancing before stopping and talking late into the night. They will always remember this birthday.

Jana says, "Greyd, I hope your birthday can compare because this one will be hard to top."

He answers, "No, I think all I want is dinner and dessert. Do you think my mom will just go with that?"

"No!" they all answer at once. Jana, Asa, and Kayden text their parents and let them know they're watching movies and staying with Greydan and JoeJoe tonight and will see them tomorrow.

38

WRAPPING IT UP

*S*aturday morning comes too quickly for the teens, and they lay around. Then they get restless and have the idea to go to the diner and see what's going on, and maybe go to the park or for a drive. When they drive over the bridge going home, Jana shivers and says, "That is the creepiest feeling, do you feel that sometimes, Elf Boy?"

"Yes, especially in the Sayer's boat house. Maybe it's just the water, and it is so cold right now."

Maybe," Jana says.

"Jana, I don't think it is your imagination," Asa says.

"Thank you for that. Sometimes I feel like I'm just making stuff up, then when it happens, I wish I had paid better attention."

"I know what you mean, we have you covered." Jana is so glad he said that. They're definitely stronger together. She's not sure what she would do without them. All of them.

Her hair blows back from her face as she's getting out of the truck. Asa doesn't have to ask what's wrong. He just reaches for her and pulls her in close as her body begins to shake. He meets Greydan's eyes over his truck, and the boys move to cover them, so no one sees, and if they do they will just see a couple in love hugging. Jana tucks her face in the crook of Asa's neck and trusts him to take care of her. She had just said she wished she paid better attention, and that is what she thinks as she moves into the vision.

She sees a beautiful watchtower. The water is churning in front of it. The day is warm. Very different from the weather of today. She notices a young couple running in the field hand in hand and laughing. Then the tower turns dark, and there's a storm. The water is black as night until the waves burst up with white froth. Again, she sees the couple. This time instead of the happy, loving way they were before, they're older and not touching. The man jerks his head up as if he can see Jana and points a skeletal finger at her and says, "It is hidden, and you shall never possess it. It's mine, and I'll kill anyone who looks."

The vision is gone as if turned off by a switch. Jana is clutching onto her Elf Boy and kisses him on the neck, pressing her hot body into his. She hears him as if he's far away. He says, "Honey, wake up we're in the parking lot of the diner, and I have you. You're safe, and I saw it like I was there. I know what you saw. You weren't and are not alone."

She moans and reaches for a kiss which he gives her willingly, but then he back up as she reaches for his belt. "Jana, hun, you need to look at me," he says. She squints as she recognizes concern on his face.

"Asa, did you understand what that evil old man was saying?"

"I heard him, but I don't know what he was talking about. Is this what happens every time you see a vision? I feel like I'm on fire, and if we were alone, it would be next to impossible to stop from making love to you."

That snaps Jana out of it more, and she giggles at him and says, "Now you know. You should tell the others how hard it is to stop, so they know I'm not doing this to hurt them, but that it's a real need."

I promise you that is precisely what I'll do. Let's go inside, and I'll tell them the entire vision and type it into your phone before we forget. I think this is something we really need to watch out for."

They go into the diner and tell the others in quiet tones where no one else can hear what she saw. They are so quiet they don't even use the car code. No one is close to their table anyway. They all think it's important and try to imagine what it could mean, but no one knows. That's usually what happens they have no idea until it happens, and it always happens. They never assume what it could mean, because from experience, they know that their guesses aren't ever what happens.

Now that they have the vision documented and saved they'll watch, awaiting that day's events. It could take days, months, or even years. The crew never worries about it; they will face it together when it gets here. Until then, they are ordering cheeseburgers and watching Asa eat five of them. Afterward, they will go to the park. Someone at the next table says there's a fair at the park, and today is as good of a day for rides and caramel apples if there ever were one. They perk up and know where they are going next, taking it one step at a time. They have lots of time.

Acknowledgements

Thank you, fans and readers our books. We appreciate each and every one of you. Please, if you enjoyed the books consider leaving us a review. It means more than you can imagine! But if you really hate them ... please pass.

We owe a great debt of thanks to an overwhelming number of people. First our families. Without your love and support, our work wouldn't be possible, nor would it be half the fun.

To those of you who call us friends, thank you for the innumerable ways in which you offer your support. We know that you chose us as friends, or in some cases, you still willingly accept the bribes we pay for not renouncing us. JK

To our frenetically fanatical females and fellows who follow us at Miki and Mine Guys and Goyles, as the gargoyles would say, "You Rock!"

Christina and Brenda, you're the best PAs ever!

To those who helped us assemble this book—Christina Schneider-Cover, and Michelle Hoffman-Editing, thank you. The work you did is invaluable and most appreciated.

To everyone else, we love you. Thank you for your support!

Miki & Garrett Ward

OTHER BOOKS BY MIKI AND GARRETT
WARD

The Ceorfan Gargoyles Series

Carved

Etched

Coming in the Series

Hewn

Shivers Series

We See You - Amazon

We See You - Nook...

We See You - Kobo

Double Mirror

Elser Books are stand alone

Flesh & Bold

Stand Alones

The Phantom Queen

Find Us @ Miki & Mine tags
Facebook group
Bookbub
Pinterest
Twitter
Instagram
<u>Miki Booksprout</u>
Miki Ward -FB or Amazon
Garrett V. Ward -FB or Amazon